The Lyon's Roar

Should I write about the strange Manteo and how he
comes and goes, slipping through our encampment,
sometimes aloof, sometimes toiling side by side with the
men as they prepare the boats for sailing? Should I tell
of my feelings whenever I see him? I'm not sure what I
feel, a certain quickening of the blood, a start of breath
held, then released. It's not the strange stirrings inside
whenever I see George, the longing of my youth, as
Eleanor describes it, to be a woman loved
and cherished.
Should I tell of how I think he sometimes watches me,
though it must surely be my imagination? These are
thoughts I can never reveal to another. One thing I
know for certain. I can have no bond with any Savage in
this wild and untamed land.

The Lyon's Roar

M.L. Stainer

Illustrated by James Melvin

Chicken Soup Press, Inc.

Circleville, New York

Chicken Soup Press, Inc.
P.O. Box 164
Circleville, NY 10919

Library of Congress Cataloging-in-Publication Data

Stainer, M.L., 1939-
The Lyon's roar / M.L. Stainer ; illustrated by James Melvin
p. cm. -- (The Lyon saga)
Includes bibliographical references.
Summary: Fourteen-year-old Jess relates her sea voyage with other English families to Roanoke Island in 1587, their attempt to make a permanent settlement, and Jess's contact with the Croatoan Indians.
ISBN 0-9646904-2-X (hardcover : alk. paper). --
ISBN 0-9646904-3-8 (pbk. : alk. paper)
1. Roanoke Colony (N.C.)--Juvenile fiction. [1. Roanoke Colony (N.C.)--Fiction. 2. America--Discovery and exploration--English--Fiction. 3. Indians of North America--Fiction.] I. Melvin, James, ill. II. Title. III. Series.

PZ7.S78255Ly 1997
[Fic]--dc21
97-2128
CIP
AC

Book design by Netherfield Productions, Pine Bush, New York
Printed by Worzalla, Stevens Point, Wisconsin
10 9 8 7 6 5 4 3 2 1

To my father, William Stainer,
who taught me to love books.

Contents

Author's Note

The author wishes to note that some spellings of familiar names have been changed according to how they are listed on original documents.

Croatoan is pronounced Cro-ah-tu-WAN; Manteo, MAN-tee-o; Ananyas, An-na-NEE-yus; Akaiyan, Uh-KY-yun; and Towaye, TOH-way.

A special note of thanks to:
Joe Mobley of the North Carolina Dept. of Cultural Resources, and Stephen Massengill of the Division of Archives and History, North Carolina Dept. of Cultural Resources, for their kind help: to Donna Fraser for her help with the cover design: to Robert Peay and Gregory MacAvoy for their proofreading assistance: to Stella Denton, Judith Alessi and Lisa Silverberg of the Pine Bush Schools' library system, and to Fran O'Gorman of Goshen library, for their help in research: to Ricardo Carballal for his assistance with Spanish: and to Kathleen McFall, Myrna Calabrese and Jane Dawkins for their invaluable criticism and encouragement.

Tuskeruro dialect: from *A New Voyage to Carolina,* by John Lawson, edited by Hugh Talmadge Lefler. Copyright © 1967 by the University of North Carolina Press. Used by permission of the publisher.

The Names of the 1587 Virginia Colonists: from *The First Colonists: Documents on the Planting of the First English Settlements in North America, 1584-1590,* by David B. Quinn and Alison Quinn. Raleigh: North Carolina Dept. of Cultural Resources, Division of Archives and History, 1982. Used by permission of Oxford University Press.

Prologue

THE 1500'S IN ENGLISH HISTORY were years of intrigue and conspiracy. By the time Henry VIII died in 1547, he'd left behind three heirs. The oldest was Mary Tudor, daughter of his first marriage to Catherine of Aragon, a Catholic whose parents were Ferdinand and Isabella of Spain. The second was Elizabeth, daughter of Anne Boleyn, Henry's second wife. His only son, Edward, was born to Jane Seymour, whom Henry married after Anne's execution. Henry left the throne to Edward, who was a sickly child from birth. Edward died in 1553, and Mary Tudor ascended the throne. Known as "Catholic Mary," also "Bloody Mary," she angered her subjects by marrying her cousin, Philip II of Spain, who became coruler of England for a short time. Mary died in 1558, leaving behind a bloody trail of martyred Protestants. When Elizabeth became Queen in 1558, the realm was divided and suspicious of the new ruler.

But Elizabeth I was her father's daughter. She restored the Anglican faith and brought about many reforms. She was encouraged to look toward the lands across the western ocean, first as a new route to the Orient; secondly, as a way to add wealth and power to her empire. English colonization was encouraged and supported, many people viewing the New World as a safe haven against problems at home. By the early 1580's, England's plan was to gain political and economic power over her Catholic adversary, Spain. Any attempts to thwart this plan met with the Queen's immediate anger. Elizabeth imprisoned and later executed her cousin, Mary Stuart, the grandniece of Henry VIII. Known as Mary Queen of Scots, she not only aligned herself with the French by marrying a dauphin, but she sought to re-establish the alliance with Philip II. Throughout all this intrigue, men of power and influence surrounded Elizabeth, constantly seeking her favor. Among them was Walter Ralegh, (Raleigh) who headed a circle of powerful and wealthy men.

Several early attempts to establish colonies in America proved unsuccessful, because they were really military garrisons and could not sustain themselves. It was Ralph Lane who first realized that in order for a colony to survive, it should be the permanent home for men, women and children who had a stake in its future.

The first explorers sent by Ralegh landed in North Carolina's Outer Banks in 1584. A garrison was created in 1585, then the entire area was explored and named Virginia for England's Virgin Queen. Spain, their chief rival under Philip, continually sought to lay its own claim upon the new lands, establishing as its primary garrisons, St. Augustine in Florida, and Santa Elena (present-day Tybee Island). The Spanish also sought to establish a colony at Chesapeake Bay, which they called "Bahia de Santa Maria."

The colony which was left on Roanoke Island in 1587 was originally intended for a landing at Chesapeake Bay to the north. Trouble between the ship's pilot, Simon Fernandes, and the captain of the Red Lyon, John White, erupted as soon as the colonists sighted Hatteras. Fernandes, who wanted nothing more than to plunder Spanish ships, literally "dumped" the entire colony on Roanoke. As winter approached, the colonists realized the precariousness of their situation and persuaded John White to return to England for supplies and reinforcements. They expected him to return within the year.

Continued sightings of Spanish ships and hostile Indians from the north contributed to their fear and apprehension. Historians speculate that some of them decided to take the remaining pinnace and sail north to their original destination. Those who remained on Roanoke counted on their friendship with the Croatoan Indians to see them through.

This is their story.

Chapter One

The Voyage

"GET BELOW, JESS," Father cautions Thomas and me. "We're setting sail."

Thank the good Lord, I think. We've been almost a full day on this ship and not a rope has slipped from its mooring. I grab Thomas's hand, much to his chagrin, and we both descend the rough-planked steps. Thomas keeps trying to peek out but I drag him with me.

"Come on," I tell him. "Father says we must wait until we're clearly out to sea."

"All right for you," Thomas pouts. "You're a girl. I don't see why I can't be up there with the men."

I laugh out loud.

"You're not a man," I remind him smugly. "You're only eleven."

And then, when I see the anger in his eyes,

"Almost a man, but we must obey Father's wishes."

And so we wait in the cramped quarters set aside for our

1

family, listening to the harsh cries of the seamen above, the groanings of the ship and the rasping of the great iron anchor as it's raised from the dark-gray depths of the water.

Already I feel somewhat seasick from the pitch and roll of our stout wooden vessel, but I vow not to give in. That would only label me, at fourteen, still a child and worse, a female who can't stomach the roil of the waves. I swallow hard and content myself with imagining what the voyage will be like. I'm trembling with excitement. How will it feel, sailing across the mighty ocean to a new world? The trip promises to be a long one, at least six to eight weeks. Will we run out of food and water? Will some mighty creature rise from the depths to wrap its tentacles around the hull and drag us under? Will we meet a Spanish ship upon the waters and be forced to heave-to? Or worse, will we be split asunder by a Spanish cannon?

I keep these musings to myself, having promised Mother not to frighten my younger brother. I find the precious sheets of paper she's given me and search for the quill pen so I can begin writing my thoughts down. Perhaps, when I'm an old woman, I'll find these pages curled and yellowed at the bottom of some dusty drawer, to read and remember this brave adventure in the year of our Lord, anno Domini, 1587.

The ship is moving. I can feel the heave and pitch as it leaves Portsmouth dock, heading not for the outer seas but toward Cowes on the Isle of Wight. I still don't understand why we have to stop there first, though Father has said that our captain, John White, is to meet with a George Carey to discuss matters which will face us in the New World. This meeting is of great concern, Father says, to review the plans of Sir Walter Ralegh, patron and sponsor of our voyage.

"I saw Sir Walter dockside at Portsmouth," Thomas

leans over to whisper in my ear as he watches me write.

"He looked most important and wore silk ruffles. He was waving his arms and yelling at the ship's pilot."

"It's his money which is financing this entire voyage," I reply. Certainly, a man like Sir Walter Ralegh is owed a great deal of respect, not only for his wealth but for his unique vision as well. Father talks often of Ralegh's dream to found a colony in the Americas, where men, women and children can carve out a new empire for the glory of our beloved Queen and England. We're to be part of that dream, we and one hundred thirteen other brave colonists. It's said that Sir Walter Ralegh has the Queen's favor, and that both are bound and determined to see Englishmen rooted in the western lands ahead of Spain. "We're to be a part of history," Father keeps saying over and over, giving Mother and me unexpected hugs.

Father's boots pound down the steps.

"Jess, Thomas, come up," he calls in his deep voice. "Come up and see the coast of England fall away and turn your gaze toward our future."

We bound up the steps and into the gray, fine rain which is coming down. It's dank and chill and a mist salts our faces, but I'm filled with much gladness and joy.

Chapter Two

First Journal

WE'VE BEEN AT SEA FOR TEN DAYS now and for most of the time, I've been too sick even to want to go on deck. The rain has fallen almost constantly since leaving Cowes. The seas are rough and the Red Lyon, our flagship, rocks ominously from side to side, breaching the waves and making it difficult to stand or walk in any direction.

I've been hard pressed to keep any food down and Mother seems worried. She puts a damp cloth to my forehead and gives me small sips of water but, in truth, I'm not disposed toward eating. Thomas, of course, has no problem with food. He gobbles it down and the sight is enough to make me sick, even if I weren't already ill. The only other girl on board, Agnes Harvye, is seven and also sea-sick.

I wonder how our ship can hold so many people. Sailing upon it and our companion flyboat, are a total of ninety-one men, seventeen women and nine children. Then there's the crew on each ship, "scurvy bunches," as Father calls them, making sure I'm never alone on those few occasions I've been deckside. Behind these two sails a pinnace of much smaller size, breaching the wake of our waves.

Last night, I overheard Father telling Mother how concerned he is about the disposition of our ship's pilot and navigator, Simon Fernandes and our captain, John White. They've been at each other's throats since the voyage began.

"There's bad-feeling between those two," he muttered, then looked around quickly to see if I'd heard. But I pretended to be writing in the corner, straining my eyes in the dull light of the oil lamp. I saw Mother put a finger to her lips and so the conversation ended. But I knew of the feud, who on board didn't, and could often hear the voices of the pilot and the captain raised in anger.

"There'll be much to do once we arrive," Father turned to his next favorite topic. "Timber will have to be cleared and houses built."

"You're a good carpenter, Arnold," replied my mother in her calming manner.

"I've plans for several dwellings," Father continued enthusiastically. "John White has assured me there are rich forests for the taking at the Baye of Chesapeake."

I wrote on my sheet of paper in large letters, "WE ARE EAGER TO SAIL AND LAY CLAIM TO THIS NEW LAND FOR OUR GOOD QUEEN, ELIZABETH I." Then I added, "BEFORE SPAIN, OUR ENEMY, DOES SO." I almost crossed out the latter, but decided to leave it there so it would remind me of the importance of our mission. Then Mother got her Bible and made me put down my papers so we could spend the remaining evening time in prayers.

I've been eyeing the boys on this voyage, though surreptitiously, I must admit. Including Thomas, there are seven of them, varying in age from eleven to sixteen. Most of them don't seem to suffer sea-sickness at all and, in fact, swagger about the deck as if they own the ship. It's disgusting how the younger ones wolf down large quantities of food, while I and Agnes, poor dear, retch unceasingly and bring up bile of the most foul color. A kindly crewman told my mother that it was just a matter of time before I got my "sea legs," as he called them. I don't know what these "legs" are, but evidently they enable the older boys and everyone else to go rollicking around without a care.

The young girl, Agnes, looked for them beneath her this morning but I merely laughed. Was she expecting a new set to grow from her body? I'm not as stupid as that. In fact, after morning prayers today, I'm feeling much better. I'll try to eat my breakfast as soon as I've finished my writing. I'll not allow my stomach to have the upper hand.

I count my sheets of paper and decide to plan my scribing for every third day. I'm so glad that Mother, in her infinite wisdom, taught me my letters for it's rare that a female can write her thoughts. Indeed, most of our fair sex, and even most males, can neither read nor write a single word. But Mother is always voicing her desire for Thomas and me to be well-educated, and Father has no objections to it. If I use both sides of a sheet, they should last throughout the voyage and leave me enough for anything I wish to write as we establish our colony. I'm certain I'll not run out of thoughts.

Chapter 3

Young George Howe

"OH, MOTHER, I'M DYING!"

"Hush, now. You're far from dying."

"Then, what is it?"

"My darling Jessabel. You're becoming a woman."

If this is what becoming a woman means, I hate it with a passion! I'm wracked with cramps and back pain. Mother smiles and brings me Mistress Steueens's hot tea and honey. She bids me rest with a pillow beneath my legs. Thomas makes faces and goes up on deck. I'm embarrassed to tears. Not even my dear Father should see me in such a condition.

I've been confined to quarters for five long days. Mother absolutely refuses to allow me to go deckside while my menses flows. She keeps Thomas and Agnes away, though all Agnes wants to do is have me read to her. Thomas keeps poking his head in and calling out gleefully, "The sun is shining gloriously," and "You should smell the fresh air," while I languish in the depths below. Mother has constructed a privacy screen so I can administer to myself without prying eyes. She's so solicitous.

But I can't stand it! I wish to be walking the deck, talking with Ambrose, John and especially, young George Howe. He's sixteen and rather nice looking. He has kind eyes and a gentle manner about him. John and Ambrose are just about fourteen, and still play silly games with Thomas and the other younger boys. But I like to talk to George Howe. Just when I'm getting to know him, this "affliction" strikes. Life is so unfair!

Today it's cloudy and cool but even so, Mother finally relents and tells me I can go on deck for some fresh air.

"You're looking so pale," she says, a worried look upon her face. Dear Mother, she has so many concerns: watching out for Thomas and his boisterous ways; making sure her daughter doesn't get into trouble; overseeing young Agnes almost as a second mother. Mistress Harvye is well-advanced with child on this voyage, as is Eleanor, the pretty young wife of Ananyas Dare. Both of them try to hide their condition, though I don't understand why. Since Mistress Harvye has no real inclination to watch Agnes, Mother has undertaken that responsibility. I must confess, I think she likes having a young daughter around once more. I'm growing up so rapidly.

Wicked Thomas! He's been such a beast these past days while I was confined below, nagging and teasing me, making silly faces. How glad I am to see him at the other end of the deck, watching the men rig the sails. George Howe is standing by the rail.

"Hello, Jess," he says quite boldly, then immediately turns bright red.

"Hello yourself, George Howe," I reply, then turn my attention to the sea and the spell of the water rolling endlessly in all directions.

"It looks like rain again," he says. "We're in for some bad weather."

I look to where he's pointing at the black thunderheads sweeping in from the west. Already, a dull rain is starting and the sun is quickly hidden behind clouds.

"This voyage brings nothing but rain," I remark glumly.

"You missed the sun," George says. "It was quite beautiful for several days. We saw some fish dancing upon the waters."

"So Thomas informed me."

George wraps his cloak more tightly around him.

"It's best we go below," he says. "This promises to be a storm of some magnitude."

"Oh, I'm sick of storms," I pout, stamping my foot. Then, realizing how I must appear to George, add contritely,

"Of course, Father said the rain will constantly replenish our water supply."

"We'll have to keep reminding ourselves of that," laughs George as we gather Thomas and the others and go below.

The rain continues steadily for several days. The Lyon roars against the waves, plunging her prow deep, then arching high. Every once in a while she gives a long shudder as the waves seize her tightly in their grip. I'm terribly afraid we'll capsize.

"You're not to worry about such things, little Jess," Father says, surprising me with a smile and a brush of his hand against my cheek.

"The sea is our friend, guiding us toward a new and wondrous future."

How amazed I am at his poetic soul! When I tell Mother, she says that men who work with wood are true poets just like the great bards, for they take the raw timber and shape it into beautiful things. After she says that, I've a new respect for my father, for I've never imagined his artistry in such a way. I give him a kiss that afternoon, embarrassing him immensely. Now, more than ever, I'm proud to be the daughter of Arnold Archarde.

Chapter 4

The Red Lyon

CAPTAIN WHITE ISN'T AT ALL WHAT I EXPECT. He's thinly built and not particularly handsome. Somehow I imagined a large burly man with a full beard and moustache, a privateer who has led many a crew to the New World. Indeed, this is exactly how Simon Fernandes, the Portuguese ship's pilot, looks.

"Just like a pirate," I whisper to Agnes, who shivers and hides behind my skirt whenever Fernandes is about.

We're being given a tour of the Red Lyon. It's all so exciting. The rain has stopped and the sun is shining against a brilliant blue sky. After a talk with Father, John White has agreed to allow us, his "living cargo," to see his great ship. What an opportunity to stay above for such a long time and feel the sun on my face. Father has cautioned me to dress conservatively and not to look any crewman in the eye. To be on the safe side, he follows us a pace or two behind.

Thomas, of course, is in his glory along with all the other

boys.

"The Red Lyon," Captain White says, "is likened in length and breadth to the same ship that Sir Richard Grenville sailed in 1585, when he first sighted land in the New World. We hope to find Grenville's original colony when we disembark."

"What happened to them, sir?" George asks.

"No one knows for sure," replies Captain White. "They were probably fallen upon by hostiles, or Spanish privateers."

George is avidly inspecting the wildfire arrows, which shoot fire when their tips are ignited. Those arrows, Captain White tells us, are similar to the ones used by the Savages against our English soldiers. I shiver when I think of being attacked while sleeping in my bed. I'm glad when Thomas drags me and Agnes to the quarterdeck gun and the bronze cannon.

"Look, Jess, look," he keeps calling. "Have you ever seen anything so big?"

"Indeed not," I smile at his enthusiasm, though guns of any kind don't appeal to me.

"What other ordnance do you have?" Ambrose and John ask together, and are shown the iron fowlers and those strange swivel guns, called "murtherers." They're each allowed to hold a firing pistol and given a piece of shot for the cannon, to feel its heavy weight in their hands.

"In my quarters are a helmet, halberd and pike," says Captain White, "which I'll show you later. The morion, for that's what the helmet is called, is a heavy piece. Our soldiers under Ralph Lane and Grenville wore those against the Spaniards. And this," he adds as we move further on our tour, "is the tiller arm by which we steer this good ship."

He points to a sturdy seaman standing in the gloom.

"This man is John Evans. He moves the whipstaff. You need to stay far away, for see his muscles. 'Tis not a job for a weakling. During a storm, it takes two to steer the whipstaff."

The man gives a low laugh and I shiver deep inside. He looks like a demon standing there, working the whipstaff amidst the dark innards of the ship. I resolve to stay far away. Captain White leads us once again into the bright sunshine.

I stare at the ship's flags blowing steadily in the wind. First is the flag of our good Queen Elizabeth, green and white for our own House of Tudor. Then flies the standard flag of England, the red cross of Saint George emblazoned on white. Finally, there's the flag of this sturdy ship, a Red Lyon imprinted against a dazzling white background. England, I suddenly think, is truly a proud fierce lyon. Tears sting my eyes.

"Lyon of England," I whisper and my throat begins to close.

Captain White calls the younger crewmen, "younkers." They're barely older than George. There's a lad standing near the mizzenmast.

"Who's that?" Thomas asks with the greatest curiosity.

"That's Will Morris, our grommet."

"Your what...?" Thomas repeats. Captain White smiles.

"Every ship has a grommet. He marks the watch and turns the hour-glass every twenty-four hours."

I stare at the boy, pale and slight of build, hardly as old as my brother. I wonder if he has a family who misses him.

"See," I whisper fiercely in Thomas's ear, "how would you like to do *that*?"

He shakes his head and pulls himself free from my grasp, then darts ahead to climb upon the cannon.

"The Lyon is one hundred and sixty tons, and one

hundred ten feet long." Captain White continues with his tour.

"Then how does it stay afloat?" Agnes asks timidly.

We all laugh, then go to view the pinnace behind us. Captain White tells us the pinnace is to be used when we arrive in the New World, to navigate the shallower seas, sounds and inlets of the coastline. We wave to Captain Stafford as he steers behind our wake.

"It looks like a rocky ride," I remark to George, watching the pinnace try to cut across the swell of the waves. George laughs.

"You'd be most sea-sick, Jess," he says.

"Then I'm glad to be on the Lyon," I comment and turn to Thomas, his legs astride the huge cannon.

"Enough," I call. "Get down from there."

The rest of the tour is uneventful and I content myself with enjoying this rare and blessed freedom: the blowing wind, the brilliant sky. When it ends, we all thank Captain White profusely and it's with deep regret that we return to our dismal quarters below.

Chapter 5

Ship's Captain

"WHY DO CAPTAIN WHITE AND SIMON Fernandes argue all the time?"

"They've been at odds since the beginning, nay, even before," Father answers.

"They're at it again," Mother whispers and, in truth, they can be heard even amidst the creakings and groanings of the ship and the wind.

"Fernandes wishes to return quickly to his privateering. He complains of losing time and money on our voyage."

"Then why did he come with us?"

"Sir Walter Ralegh paid him well for his skill in navigation and seamanship."

"He wants more," Thomas chimes in. "He's a greedy, greedy man."

Father chuckles. "He wants Sir Walter's money and more of his own. Our Thomas is right. 'Tis dreams of glittering gold that lure these seamen onward, stories of waterfalls of gold nuggets which fall continually. All one has to do is but stretch out his hands...."

Mother gasps.

"This can't be true?"

Father laughs and shakes his head.

"I strongly doubt it." Then his face grows solemn. "But what else would lure these rough men to venture upon the Western Ocean. They don't have the same dreams as we do, land promised to us and freedom to live our own lives."

"That seaman, John Evans, called this ocean an endless watery hell."

Father stares at Thomas.

"Indeed it may be," then seeing Mother's face and mine, laughs once more.

"Not a hell, but a pathway to our future." He claps Thomas on the back. "Off to bed now," he says, "and dream of golden paths."

"You must stay far away from this Simon Fernandes and the others," Mother cautions. "Oh, Arnold, I don't trust that man."

For the first time since we've left Portsmouth, I notice how worried my father looks. He's spoken several times to John White and always comes down below shaking his head, with a frown creasing his brow. Though this isn't the Captain's first voyage, it's the first time women and children have been included in such a venture. Father is most solicitous of Mother and me, and of Agnes, Mistress Harvye and fair Eleanor Dare. Every time Fernandes and the Captain argue, their bellowing rises above the wind and the waves, carrying down even into the bowels of the ship. Father is terribly unhappy but it doesn't appear that there's anything he can do.

"John White is a good man," he says, shaking his head,

"but he's not a soldier like Richard Grenville. He's allowed himself to be dictated to by the likes of Fernandes and his men."

"I just wish they wouldn't argue in front of the children," Mother whispers again. George and I are seated near. We look at each other. Neither George nor I consider ourselves children any longer. From the day of my first menses, I've felt like a true woman. My figure is growing slightly fuller and the other day, I caught George's eyes upon me. Though he glanced away quickly, his face had turned red. Inwardly, I smiled, not minding at all. Outwardly, I pretended to be angry.

George is beginning to sprout tiny hairs all over his cheeks and above his upper lip. He looks rather funny to me, but I don't say a word. George is so gentle in his way, unlike the other boys. He likes to read and often listens as I recite to Agnes. On occasion, he even picks up one of her books and reads aloud. His voice is funny, sometimes cracking in mid-sentence like one of the bullfrogs back home. Or else, it pitches high and he reminds me of a girl. Whenever that happens, George gets most embarrassed. I kick Agnes under the table and signal her not to laugh. But she's marvelously enamored of him, hanging on his every word as he reads. And I... I'm not sure.... My body is changing and love is foreign to me at this time. But I'm certain that I like George and am well content in our friendship.

Chapter 6

"Judge Not..."

THE ARGUMENTS BETWEEN FERNANDES and Captain White have continued. Their latest battle concerns our companion flyboat. When it pulled into the Bay of Portingall, Simon Fernandes kept the Red Lyon sailing ever on. He refused to turn back and lie at anchor while our escort ship made repairs to its sails.

"What a rogue," Father fumes, pacing up and down.

Even the crew is unusually tense and ill at ease. In the weeks that follow without sighting our companion ship behind us, we can all hear the sullen mutterings which hardly silence as we walk the decks:

"This endless watery hell," and, I confess, I shiver more than once. Father accompanies us everywhere, reluctant to leave us alone. In truth, I'm glad of his presence, for watching the rough men tug and pull the ropes, unfurl the sails, spit to the right and left without a thought of common decency, sends a chill through my bones. But we walk whenever Captain

White allows, for to languish in the dank and dark of the ship's bowels is too much to bear. At every eighth bell, the crew is changed, and those relieved of duty for the next four hours sleep wherever they can on the rough deck planking.

"They own naught but the clothes on their backs," George whispered to me once and I thought, what manner of men are they, to have no possessions but the sea and the sky?

Thomas watches, fascinated, as each shift of men fastens ropes and swings the mainsail to catch the wind.

"Will Edward Spicer be able to catch up, Father?"

"I don't know. We pray that our good Lord will give him a strong wind at his back once his repairs are made."

I tell Father that I think the crew should have refused to sail on. He smiles.

"We're a motley group of pilgrim passengers," he says, "with an even stranger crew of men to serve this ship. Though we should all be bound by English law and custom, that isn't always the case. But they are sworn to obey orders, otherwise they'd be considered mutinous."

"What would happen to us, Father, if the crew turned against Captain White?"

His face grows grim.

"You mustn't worry about such things," is all he says.

Mother refuses to allow me to discuss the flyboat with the other colonists on board in front of Eleanor and Margaret Harvye.

"They have enough to worry about," she cautions. "We must reach land before either one gives birth."

George and I watch the small pinnace behind us, rising and sinking its prow against the waves. It's our only escort now.

"Would the crew mutiny?" I ask.

"Possibly," George replies. "But I doubt it. Mutiny on the high seas is punishable by death, you know." He pauses. "It's not a pleasant death, Jess. Even lesser crimes carry severe penalties."

"What sort of crimes?"

"I hesitate to say."

"Oh, George," I entreat. He glances around to make sure no one is listening.

"Well, then, should a crew member murder a fellow crewman, the living man is tied to the corpse and both are thrown overboard. Should a man steal, he might be flogged or keelhauled, tied with ropes and dragged under the full length of the boat."

My mouth drops open. How many moments would be needed to traverse one hundred and ten feet under the hull of our ship? Who could survive such a dreadful punishment? Would the crewman be pulled gasping from the depths like a fish gasps in our air, sweet to us but poison to it? Or would he dangle limp from the ropes, water streaming from his mouth? I shake my head to waken from this nightmarish vision, and find George staring at me.

"What strange thoughts were you having? I saw you shaking."

"Oh, George, how do you know such terrible things?"

"I've listened and asked questions."

I shudder. "Father said that some of this crew are felons released from Colchester Castle. He calls them yokels and ale-house runagates. They were jailed for thievery. That thought doesn't please me at all."

George gives a low chuckle.

"My father said that some of our passengers were also released from Colchester. Some are former servants. We're not all blue-blooded, my dear Jess."

"It's true," Mother tells me later. "Many have been granted pardons from our beloved Queen, so they can start afresh in the New World. England is a country teeming with people. It's a way to ease our overcrowding and quickly establish our colonies. Thank the good Lord none of them are murderers, merely those who've committed thievery."

And when my mouth drops open, she takes her Bible.

"Judge not," she whispers, "that ye be not judged."

That evening at supper, Father speaks for the first time about Manteo and Towaye, the two Savages on board. He tells us how they've been brought to England from the Virginia lands to meet the Queen. Manteo speaks a rudimentary English and is to act as translator for the new colony against any other hostiles we might encounter. Towaye is his faithful companion, a holy man, says Father.

"But you shall not walk the decks when they're about," Mother quickly admonishes. "They're Heathens!"

"They've met the Queen," Father says. "And bowed before her."

"Nevertheless, I won't have Jess wandering into them."

"The younger boys flock to them like flies to honey," I protest.

But Mother is adamant.

"You must spend more time with Eleanor Dare," she says firmly. "She's growing weary of her confinement and could use some company. It's our most fervent prayer that her babe and Mistress Harvye's will be born on land, not on this turbulent sea. You'll find her sweet and companionable. She is, after all, only about five years older than you, dearest Jess. You might be sisters."

Chapter 7

The Storm

OH, I'VE GROWN SO WEARY of this voyage. It's become loathsome and I don't know if we can all stand it. We don't have proper beds to sleep in, only the roughest spots wherever we can find a corner for our pallets. Most families try to keep together, but last night Thomas kicked me full in the face with his foot. He was sleeping and didn't remember a thing the next day when I told him about it.

There's no privacy anywhere. Our toilet is a bucket and water hauled from the side of the ship. Father has rigged a canvas cloth around the area, but it's hardly fitting. My menses came again, only nineteen days after the last, a fact not uncommon in young girls, Mother assures me. She feels our diet has something to do with it.

If I eat any more fish with moldy biscuits, I'll surely vomit all my food. The hardtack we've been eating got wet and became full of crawling maggots. On rare occasions, we've been apportioned some oatmeal but even that has become scarce. There aren't any more fruits or vegetables left. I ache for the succulent sweetness of an orange.

Last night, Father allowed Thomas to sleep on deck with George and some of the other boys. He rigged a canopy over one small part of the deck near the mast and they slept under a crescent moon.

"Why can't I sleep on deck, too, Father? Why can't I, why can't I?"

But he absolutely forbade it and I didn't dare ask again.

So I'm a prisoner in spite of my womanhood and years over Thomas. Mistress Eleanor consoles me as best she can. She's really very sweet. To ease my frustration, she lets me feel the child kicking inside her. She takes my hand and places it upon her high rounded belly. I hold my breath. The child gives a mighty heave and kicks right under where my hand is.

"It's alive," I gasp, then feel very foolish.

"Of course it is," she laughs. "Very much so." She gives a prolonged sigh.

"I'm afraid if we don't sight land soon, my poor babe will be born amidst these rough planks and even rougher men."

I feel very badly for her. Master Ananyas has made a special place for her near to us where she can rest in private. Mother stays close by now, dividing her time equally between her and Mistress Harvye, leaving Agnes in my care. Mistress Harvye is older than Eleanor, at least twenty-eight and this is her second confinement. But she hasn't been well since the voyage began and I know that Mother is worried.

"I'm greatly concerned about both women," she tells Father. "They're coming to term and this is no place to birth a child."

"Children have been birthed in worse places," he answers. "We'll do the best we can."

I know then that he went to talk in private with Captain White, but what became of that talk was not discussed in front of me.

A monstrous storm almost ends our voyage two days later. We pray mightily for God's intervention and spend most of the time bailing out our leaking ship.

I can hear the crew running about above deck and below, trying to locate the seepage. During the storm we stay below, of course; not even Father dares venture topside. The Lyon dips her prow deep into the waves which wash over her decks in an alarming manner. Then she lunges up and stands almost perpendicular to the water. The planking creaks with severity and shudders continuously. The howl of the wind reaches our ears even below. I'm terribly afraid.

The air where we are turns most vile, filled with the stench of vomit, feces and urine. The slop buckets overturn, the water swirls frighteningly around my ankles. The men work their never-ceasing battle against the sea. Mother looks worried as she tends to Mistresses Harvye and Eleanor, who are both green with sea-sickness. Last night, I gave an awful scream as three rats scurried across the water-soaked floor. Though the rats are our constant companions on this voyage, I've never seen any but only heard their squealings and chittering behind the planks.

"What's the matter?" Father came running.

"Oh, look, look, do you see them?"

"They're gone now," he said, glancing around. "The filthy things are drowning themselves in the planking. Come now, my Jess isn't afraid of some rats?"

"Are we going to capsize?" I asked fearfully. He smiled.

"John White and Simon Fernandes, though at odds, are

among the best seamen in the fleet. There's nothing to worry about. The Lyon is a sturdy vessel and has weathered many such storms. We'll all live to tell about this one."

Then he gave me a surprising hug, just like he used to do when I was a child sitting on his knee. I felt better and soon after, the sea grew calmer, the Lyon rocked less and the water level on the floor started to go down.

Chapter 8

Mistress Eleanor

MISTRESS HARVYE SCARES EVERYONE tonight by going into a false labor. I've no idea there is such a thing. She begins wailing with fear and pain and Mother runs immediately to her side.

"Take Agnes to Mistress Steueens," she whispers to me, "then come back and assist."

"Oh, Mother, will she die?"

There's no answer and so I do as I'm bid, glad to deliver a frightened Agnes into Mistress Steueens's capable hands. When I go back to see Mother, she's wiping a damp cloth over Mistress Harvye's face while the poor woman grips her hand like an iron clamp. I can see the rock-hardness of her belly.

"She must be hurting you," I whisper, seeing Mother's knuckles white in the grasp.

"No matter," says Mother, continuing her ministering.

"Will she die?" I ask again, fearfully.

"Silly girl, always afraid of dying. No, Jess. Mistress

Harvye isn't going to give birth yet. The babe is too high and she has at least another two months. But sometimes women in their last stages of confinement experience a birthing pain that seems almost real. Most often, it goes away."

"Then she isn't having her child?"

"I don't think so," comments my very wise mother but to be on the safe side, she bids me stay close at hand, ready to summon the physician if needed.

We wait with Mistress Harvye through a long night and just before dawning, she falls into a deep sleep. The contractions have stopped and Mother is then able to relax. Her poor hand looks crushed.

"Shall I fetch the doctor," I ask, bringing her a cup of hot tea that Mistress Steueens has brewed.

"For Mistress Harvye?" Mother questions, sipping the honey tea. She looks exhausted.

"For you and your poor hand," I answer, kissing her cheek. We both begin to laugh.

And if that isn't enough excitement aboard the Lyon, we sight sea birds the next day, flying off the starboard bow. It's the fifty-fourth day since we left Portsmouth on April twenty-six, and the wind has risen.

"It's a sign of approaching land," exclaims Father, giving Mother and me big hugs. "We must be nearing the islands of the West Indies."

"Oh, I'm so thankful," she cries, and she gives both me and Thomas a kiss. He's jumping up and down with joy and doesn't seem to notice her affection.

Even Mistress Harvye seems to take great heart from the news. She sits up in her bed, forgetting the contractions of yesterday, and claps her hands together in glee. Mistress Eleanor is also greatly delighted.

"My babe will be born in the New World," she smiles, and I smile back, for Mother has told me that both of them still have several weeks more of their confinement.

It seems to me that making a child is not a difficult task, though delivering one might well be. I was told this by my friends back in London. Mary and Alice didn't go into any details but they surely giggled a great deal. I've not yet had the courage to ask Mother, though Mistress Eleanor has hinted at tenderness and love shared between a man and a woman. Though fourteen, I'm still ignorant of all the facts. I'm learning, however, about carrying the results of such tenderness and intimacy, for Eleanor has let me feel her babe's movements on several occasions. I've even been able to trace the outline of its little body.

"That's a foot," she says when it kicks just under her ribs.

"How do you know?"

"Well, it must indeed be a foot, for it has great force and my ribs are sore."

"Does it hurt badly?"

"No, no," she replies with a smile. "There's some pressure and oftentime, I have trouble sleeping in certain positions, but it doesn't hurt. Carrying a child is an act of love."

I thought about it for a minute.

"I have trouble sleeping in certain positions too, especially when I find Thomas's foot almost in my mouth."

We both laugh out loud.

"You've passed into your menses?" she continues with a slight blush. I nod, blushing equally. Rarely have I even talked with Mother about such things.

"The cramping you feel at that time must be similar to what I sometimes feel."

She reaches over and takes my hand. At that moment, I feel especially close to Mistress Eleanor.

"Are you frightened to bring forth your child?"

"It's my first. Sometimes a woman's first birthing is difficult. Still," she adds, reassuring both me and herself, "I've your capable mother at my side, my dear Ananyas and our worthy physician."

I don't have much time to continue talking with her, for Mother calls me to come close as a wind squall is approaching.

Chapter 9

First Love

"JESS, JESS," CALLS THOMAS. "Come quickly. We're passing some islands. Hurry up!"

I run up as quickly as I can to see us sailing between the isle of Guadalupe and another called Dominica.

We can see them in the distance. When I close my eyes, I can almost smell the rich sweet land. The crew gives a mighty cheer that seems to shake the very timbers of the Lyon.

"No matter," laughs Father. "Isn't this a splendid sight?"

"You must see for yourself," exclaims Mother, helping Mistress Harvye to the rail so she can view the distant shapes. Mistress Eleanor is holding fast to her husband, Ananyas. Her child won't be born at sea after all.

"Can we heave to, Father? When will we land? Oh, I do so want to set foot on firm ground again."

"Not so impatient, Jess. Captain White is talking to Fernandes right now. Let's wait and see."

But it appears that Simon Fernandes won't allow the Lyon to drop anchor and once again, he and the captain are in heavy argument. So we sail right through and past those fair isles and continue at sea for another two days.

It doesn't seem right to me that Captain White submits so easily to the will of this other man. I think Fernandes is a brute, given to rude ways and manners. Father said one time that he suspects John White is intimidated by him and perhaps that's so. Nevertheless, we're all bitterly disappointed.

To cheer us up, Father says we can all sleep on deck tonight. He rigs a larger canvas to make a shelter. Mother and I are elated. We ask Mistress Harvye and fair Eleanor Dare to join us. Eleanor declines, blushing modestly as she tells us she prefers to spend this night in seclusion with her husband.

Mother understands, for privacy has been long missing from our voyage. But Mistress Harvye and Dyonis are glad to be included as part of our family. We all sing as we shake out the musty bedding and let them air dry. Tonight, Father promises, we will sing some more and tell stories.

"Sit here." I make room for Mistress Harvye. She gives me an appreciative smile, easing down to her place by our side. Master Dyonis is gentle and concerned. I think then that husbands of wives who are with child are most solicitous of their feelings. Mother catches me staring at the two of them.

"Stop," she whispers. "It's impolite."

But it makes me feel good just to watch them. At first, Agnes snuggles close to me, then leaves to sit by her mother and father. It's then that George signals me to go below to help him fetch the rolled up cushions we use as pillows.

I almost choke on the dank air. To think that we've lived and breathed it in for so many weeks. The air above is so different and full now of the scent of the land. I almost imagine I can smell flowers.

"You're like a flower," says George suddenly, and his voice sounds all funny.

I blush, though he can't see it.

"I'm no flower, George Howe," I remark, bending to pick up a cushion.

"Oh yes, you are the flower of my heart." And he pulls me awkwardly toward him, holding me fast. I can feel his beating heart and I smell the smell of him, manly, mingled with sweat. It isn't unpleasant. He leans his cheek against mine, his whiskered skin prickling.

"What if Mother or Father...?"

"Why, we're doing nothing wrong."

"We can't be here," and I start to push him away.

"Oh, Jess, all these long days and weeks I've seen you, lived close to you, watched you walk. It's been unbearable."

He sounds so pathetic, I almost laugh.

"You're so silly, George," I say, trying to make light of it.

"Love isn't silly. I... love you, Jess."

He holds me tight, then pulls away as if burned by fire. Strange that my own heart is beating fast within me. I fight against it.

"We mustn't...."

"Oh, Jess... Jess...," and then he turns and flees up the planked steps to the deck above, leaving me miserably alone.

Chapter 10

Paradise

TODAY, WE ANCHOR OFF AN ISLAND named Santa Cruz.
We hasten toward land in our small boats and finally feel solid
ground beneath our feet.

What a strange feeling not to be on a ship. In truth, the
ground rises up to meet me and I almost stumble, were it not
for Father holding my arm.

"Be careful," he warns. "The ground is shaky for me,
also."

"Why do we all feel so badly?"

Father laughs.

"Though we're on land, our bodies still think we're at
sea. We're accustomed to the tilt and roll of the Lyon, and so
we still move with her."

I watch Mistress Harvye being carried ashore by Dyonis,
and Eleanor staggering as she leans heavily on Ananyas's
arm. The ground keeps rocking and I feel dizzy and weak.

"It's an awful feeling."

"It will pass. And now, my daughter, see what you can do to help Mistresses Harvye and Dare."

We gather in small clusters, talking softly but with much enthusiasm.

"Is this Virginia?" Thomas asks Father, excitedly.

"No. We still have a way to travel. The land named for our Virgin Queen is much further north. We're here to replenish our water and supplies."

The men form small groups, while the women huddle together in clusters. Already, Simon Fernandes and John White are engaged in another argument. Father looks up, weary from the bellowing sounds echoing down the beach, then turns his attention to other needs.

"We must search for sweet water, and find food."

"Oh, Father, may Thomas and I come with you?"

Father looks at Mother, who nods her head.

"You must stay close by me," he cautions. "We don't know for sure what lies beyond those trees."

And so, Father and some men, along with Thomas, myself, George and some of the older boys, go off to find water and supplies. A short way down the beach, other groups are forming, some with women, including a young mother with her nursing infant. We're all beginning to feel better now, filled with much excitement. Mother remains on the beach with the expectant women and some others.

"Go along," she smiles. "But stay close to Father. And watch Thomas," she admonishes.

"You must hold my hand," I tell him and, for once, he doesn't give me an argument.

We set off toward the nearby trees. What joy to breathe the clean fresh air, not fouled by smells of sweat and urine. There's an odor of citrus and sweet honey also. I take deep breaths, filling my lungs and laugh to see Thomas and the others doing the same thing. George doesn't look my way and stays on the far side of the group. I suck in my breath when I see him, remembering that moment when he held me close. Surely my face is as red as his, but I keep my head down and dutifully follow Father.

"Stay close," whispers Father as we near the trees, entering what seems to be a secret grove. Green leafy fronds spread before and above us, the sun winking through their feathery branches. There is the quiet hum of insect wings, the sounds of birds and the smell of rich earth in our nostrils. As we move deeper, we can no longer hear the crashing of the breakers upon the beach. A peace descends, a tranquility I've not experienced in many weeks. The others must feel the same way.

"Let us pray," says Ambrose Viccars as he takes off his hat. As one, we all stop and bow our heads.

"Our Father," he begins. "Which art in heaven...."

Some of the men sink to their knees upon the earthy floor; the woman with her child begins to hum softly. Even Thomas is quiet, his boyish face filled with awe.

"We've discovered paradise," Father whispers and several nod in agreement. I glance at him and see, to my wonder, tears streaking down his cheeks. My own eyes begin to fill with tears, but tears of happiness, not pain. We've succeeded in our mission, crossing that mightiest of seas with its powerful storms and demons and arriving safely upon the shores of this beautiful virgin land. We have a great deal for which to be thankful.

"Praise to our good and noble Queen Elizabeth," says another man and we all join in.

"Praise and honor to our Virgin Queen, who so inspired

us to be pilgrims on this venture. Praise to the Lord our God who, in His supreme wisdom, watched over us and guided us safely to this shore."

Then as one, we move further into paradise to seek water and nourishment for the rest of our journey.

Chapter 11

"We're Poisoned!"

AS WE MOVE DEEPER INTO THE LAND and away from the beach, hunger gnaws dully at our insides like an animal. It's been so long since we've eaten anything other than moldy biscuits and dried beef. I'm becoming dizzy again, not from the land rocking beneath me but from the ache in my stomach. Thomas breaks away from my grasp and runs with the others, crashing through the trees until I can no longer see him.

"Father?" I call, watching Thomas disappear.

"Let him go," he replies. "This isle appears uninhabited."

We walk a while longer, then I see Thomas reappear from the woodland, his hands full of what looks like small green apples.

"We found these growing on the trees. Come, everyone, they're just like the apples from home."

We rush and take some from him and the other boys. In truth, they appear just like the familiar green fruit of our beloved England. Father wants us to wait, but the men and women begin to bite into them, so we all follow suit.

Our apparent food becomes a terrible misfortune! No sooner do we begin to devour the fruit, than our mouths start burning with the most vile fire.

"What is this? What is this?" we all scream as our tongues rapidly begin to swell. Thomas and the smaller boys are badly afflicted. He starts crying and running around in pain. Try as I can, I'm not able to do a thing for him as my own mouth burns and my lips and tongue quickly swell. Some around me are so badly swollen that they can't even speak. The infant who nursed at his mother's breast is also afflicted in the same manner, having suckled her milk. He begins to cry most piteously.

"Oh! Oh!" screams Thomas and the others. "Help us, help us!" while our mouths are consumed by fire.

We all rush about gagging and spitting out the poisonous pieces. George and the older boys aren't as bad, having waited to allow the children to eat their fill. I catch a glimpse of Thomas's poor swollen features, but there's nothing anyone can do. We push our way back to the beach, gasping and choking. I'm sore afraid we're going to die.

"What is it, pray tell me what's wrong?" Mother cries, upon seeing us emerging from the trees.

"We're poisoned," Father groans, hardly able to answer her. She runs to get sweet water for us to wash out our mouths, but there's precious little.

"Give me the babe," she cries and takes the wailing infant from his mother's breast. She swabs out his tiny mouth again and again, while his poor mother sobs her eyes out.

Everyone rushes to the sea to draw the salt water into our mouths. But the salt only serves to burn us more. Soon we all just lie on the ground, moaning in torment from the pain.

If this is paradise, I think fearfully, then God has surely played a foul trick upon us. Father manages to speak enough to send some men for beer from the Lyon. They set about in the small boats to fetch it. In the meanwhile we lie around, some moaning and thrashing, others quiet in their agony, until the men come back. Even the babe is given a rag dipped in beer to ease the pain. Though it doesn't help all that much, the terrible burning eases somewhat and we're then able to gather ourselves and begin anew the search for water and unpoisoned food.

"Must you go again?" Mother places her hand on Father's arm, then stands aside as he nods and leads the way, his eyes red from the pain and tearing. Simon Fernandes stays near the shoreline, watching as John White joins Father's group. He stares angrily out to sea, refusing to help in their second search. Mother is weeping and holding Thomas close by her side. I sit by Eleanor who cries also, even though she hasn't eaten any fruit.

"Oh, dear," she keeps sobbing. "What if we don't find any food?"

"We will," I assure her, though in my heart I'm full of dread. "I know Father won't rest until he brings back food that is safe for us to eat."

And so we stay like that for the rest of the day and long into the night, the swelling and pain eventually disappearing. By dawn, when Father and the group return, most of the swellings have gone down and we've recovered.

Chapter 12

George Again

WE'VE SET SAIL FROM SANTA CRUZ, for it's an island certainly not hospitable to us. After we'd recovered from the poison fruit, we thought our fortunes had turned for the better. A group discovered five large tortoises, which were so big that it took almost sixteen of our men to carry one.

We heard them calling excitedly and watched them drag the large shelled animal down to the beach. Even I was curious at such a strange creature, not unlike the garden tortoises at home, but of such giant size that once again, Agnes hid behind me.

It was a brownish-black color, and moved so slowly that the boys could poke it with a stick and it hardly reacted.

"Stop that!" I yelled at Thomas who, like the others, was delighting in its torment. With loud "Hellos" the men kept dragging each beast down until all five were deposited on the shore. Some of the men then proceeded to club them over their heads which, unfortunately for the tortoises, couldn't be

41

drawn into their shells fast enough. I couldn't bear to watch.

When all were killed, they were boiled in their shells and the cooked meat cut out into small pieces. We all ate heartily, though my stomach churned with the thought of eating such an animal. The meat tasted tough and stringy.

The men were elated at this discovery. Some of the meat was saved and packed away for later use. There was enough so that each family could receive its share.

But more misfortune fell upon us soon after. Another group of men and women went exploring once more, finding what they thought was fresh water. Instead, it was a pond full of stagnant liquid so vile that their faces began to burn soon after they had washed in it. Within hours, their faces swelled and their eyes were forced shut.

"This isn't a good omen," Father muttered angrily and went to talk with Captain White. Upon his return, yet another party of men was dispatched to climb to the top of a high hill where they could survey the island. Later, they told us they saw signs that Savages had once lived there, and one man claimed to see some slipping through the trees.

Most fortunately, they also discovered a spring of fresh running water and were able to fill containers to carry it back to those of us waiting on the beach.

"Thank goodness," Mother exclaimed, giving each of us a drink of pure sweet water. I'd never tasted anything so delicious in all my life. We drank our fill thankfully, careful to give all due praise to God. With both meat and water, we were then able to replenish our supplies for the next part of our journey.

Captain Stafford and the pinnace have already left ahead of us, searching for sheep which Simon Fernandes claims are on another island. When we arrive at the destination where

he's anchored, we find that Fernandes has been ill-advised of his facts. There are no sheep or animals of any kind. We resign ourselves to eating tortoise meat and set sail once again, heading toward Musketas Baye.

At least we have fresh water on board and a supplementary food supply. But to be back at sea with the squeaking rats is almost more than I can bear.

"Oh, Mother, will this trip ever end?"

She kisses my cheek.

"As bad as it is for us," she answers, "it's worse for Margaret Harvye and Eleanor." Indeed, Eleanor weeps quietly when she thinks no one is looking, and Mistress Harvye has taken to her bed again, refusing to see even Dyonis. Only Mother goes near to bring her broth and comfort.

"I don't believe in paradise," I tell Thomas firmly as we sail past other small islands. Captain White refuses to stop until he arrives at Musketas. Simon Fernandes is in one of his foulest moods. Father says he and John White have almost come to blows on several occasions, though Fernandes is surely the bigger man. He screams that he wishes to dump us all and return to his privateering and the Spanish gold he is losing. Captain White reminds him of his pledge and, especially, the use of his services paid for by Sir Walter Ralegh. Once more, my heart sinks with the worry that harm will be done.

As for George, he's avoiding me completely. Whenever he sees me, he turns and walks in the opposite direction. One time, though, he's coming down the steps as I'm going up. We almost bump foreheads.

"George," I say in surprise. "I've missed you greatly."

George stands there, struck dumb as a patient ox.

"Won't you say something?"

"There's nothing to say," he mutters, looking upset. "You've pushed me away."

"Indeed I haven't."

He turns to go back up the steps, but I grab his arm and am immediately aghast at my forward nature.

"George, I'm too... new at this game of love. I don't know all the rules. You must be... patient with me."

He hesitates, turning around.

"If that's true, Jess, then... then...."

"What?"

"... I'll be most patient." He takes my hand speedily, though I'm trembling and my palms are wet.

"Do you... still... like me?"

What am I to say? Perhaps I like him too much. Is that love? How am I to know? I finally find enough courage to answer in breathless tone.

"It's true that I like you, George Howe. And it's true that I like you a great deal. I can't answer now that I love you for I surely don't know."

There is such joy upon his face at that moment that it's as if a light shines around his head.

"Then I'll continue to be patient," he says with a soft smile, the first I've seen for a long time. "I'll be patient until you're sure, Jessabel Archarde."

And once more he turns abruptly and bounds up the steps, two at a time. I confess I don't understand the ways of the masculine heart. I would have much preferred that he kiss me!

Chapter 13

The Savage

WE'RE IN GOD'S GREAT DEBT, as we land at Musketas Baye without any blood shed between our captain and the ship's pilot. There were several moments when it seemed some of the crew would have to interfere and separate the two as they stood face to face in confrontation.

"Bloody damned Englishman," is what Simon Fernandes screamed at John White.

"Rogue and pirate," John White said in return.

Father and Ambrose Viccars went to try and talk to both of them, but it appeared useless. Back and forth they argued, with White accusing Fernandes of sabotage for not turning back to aid our stricken flyboat in Portingall, and the latter accusing our captain of weakness and misdirection. Thomas, Agnes and I kept as far away from the two of them as possible. Only the Savages, Manteo and Towaye, stayed close to the captain, for their allegiance was apparently to him in all ways.

"He scares me," I say to George.

"Who, Fernandes?"

"Yes, him. But also, the one they call Manteo. I've never seen him smile."

"Savages don't smile," comments George.

"He does," chimes in Thomas.

"Does what?"

"Smile. I saw him."

"When did you see him?"

"The other day. John and I were playing sticks. He was watching us. I saw John cheat but he denied it. The Savage smiled when I accused John and nodded his head."

"That isn't true."

"It is, it is. I saw him with my own eyes. He smiled, and I knew that John was a liar."

George pulls Thomas to his side and kneels down in front of him.

"And just what did you do after that?"

"I gathered up the sticks and told John I wouldn't play any more. The Savage was watching us. When John went away, I thought perhaps he might come over, but he didn't."

"I would think not," I exclaim with indignation.

"Hush, Jess," George says. "There was no harm in his watching them play."

"He scares me."

"Well, he doesn't scare me," Thomas says, squirming out of George's reach. "He's taught us how to whistle for birds."

"I'll tell Mother."

"Father already knows," pouts Thomas with a stubborn look. "He said it was all right."

When I go to Father and tell him, he nods his head.

"It's true," he says. "Manteo has taught the younger lads

47

to make bird sounds."

"But he's so...."

Father gives a laugh.

"He's met our beloved Queen and been at Court. Have you forgotten? It's known that she favors him."

I pout.

"You won't let me walk the decks when he's about."

Father's eyes grow hard and narrow.

"That's different," he speaks sharply. "You're a young girl and as such, must be protected at all times."

"From him?"

Father gives me a long hard look.

"From any man," he says then with such a sternness that I wonder if he means George Howe as well.

Chapter 14

More Bad Luck

"DID THEY FIND MORE WATER?"

"I tell you, they've drunk more beer than they've gathered any water."

"Oh, Arnold, what is John White going to do about this?"

"He said he can't do much until the spirits wear off."

And so, we just sit around waiting while the crew drinks itself into a stupor and the beer runs out. Father is most distressed. He and several of the men trudge off to see our captain but, in truth, there isn't much to be done until the next day.

At that time, there are moanings aplenty and the sounds of vomiting. Agnes and I just cover our ears and stay far away from where the crew languishes, while Mother purses her lips and tends to Mistress Harvye and Eleanor.

"What more bad luck can plague this voyage?" Father says bitterly but, indeed, there is more. Two of the crewmen desert, one leaving his goodwife prostrate with grief. I overhear Father tell Mother they're of Irish descent, so what can any one expect. Darby Glande's wife, Elizabeth, weeps for days after, saying she knew nothing of his plan.

"I only know," she adds through reddened eyes, "that he was imprisoned against his will by that scoundrel, John White."

Our entire group is full of ill-feeling. It's hard for any of us to imagine Captain White holding a man against his will, as she claims.

"That's simply not true," Father says most emphatically.

Angry mutterings can be heard everywhere, from crew to colonist, but no one is sure of what actually happened. Of the other man, Dennis Carroll, little is known.

So we're down two crew members and missing one small boat, which they took stealthily in the dark of night. Elizabeth Glande weeps incessantly, her eyes red and swollen, so now Mother has another person with whom to concern herself.

"Oh, George, do you think we'll ever arrive at Chesapeake to establish our Cittie of Ralegh?"

He smiles grimly, looking beyond where I'm standing to the dark sea and the waves.

"I believe we will, if only this constant feuding between White and Fernandes would stop."

He's referring to yet another battle between those two. We had intended to take on salt and further supplies at Rojo Baye, where the Spaniards have a stockpile. It was to be a clandestine raid, for we need salt desperately in order to preserve our food. Though the venture was risky at best, the pinnace was readied with many armed men. It sailed away but then, made an abrupt turnaround when Fernandes suddenly changed his mind and refused to go further.

"He's ranting like a madman," Father told Thomas,

Mother and me, watching from the Lyon's prow. "He's tearing up and down the deck. The men are waiting to see what will happen next."

It soon became evident that nothing would happen. The pinnace sailed back into the bay, and we've all agreed that Fernandes will be damned forever for taking the name of our Lord God in vain. And we are still without salt.

We've set sail again, and are now passing close along a shoreline where Captain White wishes to stop. He's hoping to gather fruit plants for our settlement: orange, pineapple, banana and other bushes. But Fernandes once more refuses to heave to. So the Lyon and its unhappy passengers continue sailing up the coast, our only consolation being that we're heading toward Virginia and an end to this interminable journey.

Chapter 15

Manteo

MOTHER SWOONS ONE LATE AFTERNOON, after being on her feet for almost the entire day.

"Jess... Jess... get your father quickly...."

He comes running, lifting her in his arms and placing her on the pallet. She's flush with fever and complains of her joints aching.

I run to get Mistress Steueens, who boldly pushes her way down the steps and takes over from my father.

"Get me some wet cloths," she commands. "And tell my Agnes to heat water for some tea. Bring some of the honey, too. Now, let's loosen this clothing and make her more comfortable."

How glad I am to see such love and concern for my dear mother. She, who has cared for Thomas and me, Mistress Harvye and fair Eleanor, and not to forget Elizabeth Glande, is herself in need of care. Mistress Steueens fusses about her like a hen with a baby chick. She clucks like one, also, shooing Thomas away to stay with George and his father.

"Give me those cloths," she orders and shows me how to sponge Mother down. I can feel the heat rising from her skin. It's dry and hot.

"Come, Mother," I plead, "sip some of this hot tea."

For three days and nights we keep a close vigil as we minister to her. The fever rages and she moans in a fitful sleep. More than once, I think her dead as she lies there so still and quiet after a night of tossing and turning. I say my prayers several times each day and read many passages from her Bible, especially the Twenty-Third Psalm.

"The Lord is my shepherd; I shall not want...."

Father comes down the steps.

"I've brought the physician," he says finally and he's there with his doctor's potions at the ready.

"This woman must be leeched," he orders, but Father just shakes his head.

"She wouldn't want leeches to suck her blood," he says sorrowfully. The physician speaks sharply.

"Wash her down with cool water and keep her quiet," he instructs.

Father and I look at one another, for that's exactly what we've been doing. After he leaves, I breathe a huge sigh of relief. Father manages a wry smile.

"We know more of doctoring than he."

Mistress Eleanor begs to come and sit with her but both Father and Ananyas won't hear of it. But after the physician has gone, Mother begins to sweat profusely, drenching the bedding and her clothes. Finally, on the fourth day, the fever breaks and she opens her eyes. I almost walk in on her and Father that evening when she's starting to feel better.

"I was so worried," I hear Father say. He's holding her

hand. "I don't know what I'd have done if..."

"Hush...," whispers Mother weakly. "Don't think of such awful things."

"Beloved," he whispers, leaning down to kiss her cheek. "I couldn't live my life without you."

I don't go in but softly creep away, leaving them alone. In all my years, I can't remember a more tender moment shared between them. I go up on deck, to lean against the rail and stare out at the ocean. The Lyon is riding smoothly this night, the stars shining in their firmament. My heart is full of love for both of them.

"You should not... be here."

And I turn to see the Savage, Manteo, standing behind me. His eyes gleam like points of silver against his brown skin. My heart jumps and I gasp, clutching my throat.

"Don't come any closer," I start to say. But he doesn't make any attempt to come nearer and only stands there in the darkness.

"You are... afraid?" His voice is resonant, with an inflection foreign to my ears. Then I realize that English isn't his native tongue. I shake my head,

"No," while my heart pounds so loudly in my chest, I think he can surely hear.

"That is... good," he says. "Manteo means you... no harm."

I rush away then, not knowing if he still stands there in the night, down the steps to the comfort and security of my mother and father. I don't tell them whom I've seen, not George, not Mistress Eleanor, indeed, not a soul. That night I sleep fitfully, dreaming of a dark-skinned man holding my hand, carrying me away in his strong, powerful arms. I can't see the man's face, but it's not George Howe.

The image of the Savage has haunted my dreams for several nights. I toss and turn, unable to sleep. As Mother grows stronger, my dreams also intensify. Last night, Thomas complained that I'd turned in my fitfulness and almost squashed him "like a bug."

My fourth menses time has come and gone. My figure continues to ripen and George is most attentive. He accompanies me everywhere, bringing a smile to Mother's lips and a frown to Father's, though he doesn't say a word. George has also grown taller, filling out his shoulders and frame. His whiskers have thickened and he looks most manly. Yesterday he turned seventeen and we had a celebration.

George Howe, the elder, invited us all to a party. There were spirits and I was allowed a sip. Father even let Thomas taste some, though he wrinkled up his nose in disgust.

"It's awful," he said and we all laughed.

George's father presented him with his watch and chain, which young George immediately put on with great reverence. Then we sang songs and made merry until Father realized how late it was and sent us all to bed.

There is a stalemate between John White and Simon Fernandes, a brooding calm which belies the hidden storm. But at least, we've had no bellowing and arguing. The peace is most welcome.

Last night, George waylaid me in a corner of the cabin and kissed me with a most passionate kiss. We'd been talking and before I knew it, his mouth was upon mine. I could hear his heavy breathing. In truth, I didn't know quite what to do, but found myself kissing him back with equal ardor.

"Oh, my beloved Jess," he whispered over and over. "I'm mad with passion for you."

We clung to each other for several moments, kissing most

impetuously. Suddenly we heard a noise behind us and both of us jumped back startled, our faces red with guilt. But we couldn't see anything, just a fleeting shadow, an illusion of someone who'd been there.

I'm unnerved. For days I've been unable to think of anything else, George's kiss and the one who was also there, watching from the shadows.

Chapter 16

Return of the Flyboat

IT'S JULY TWENTY-SECOND WHEN WE finally sail into
a calm sea of water near Hataraske and lay anchor off shore.
Captain White calls the island Roanoak and goes aboard the
pinnace with forty of his bravest men. It's their intent to go
inland and explore what was left of the former Grenville party.

"That is," says Father with a grim face. "If there's
anything to find."

We suddenly hear yelling and shouting from above and
as we rush topside, realize that the calm between our captain
and the ship's master is at an end. John White, on the pinnace,
is yelling back at Fernandes, still on the Lyon with us. It seems
that Fernandes has somehow signaled his men to leave
White's men on Roanoak once they land, returning only with
Captain White and two others.

"John White is a fool and a weakling," Fernandes cries.
"It's here you've arrived and here you'll stay!"

This is the storm which has been brewing these many

days, an open rebellion on Fernandes's part. We have no say in it; those of us remaining on the Lyon watch in fearfulness. That pirate, as Father and the others call him, uses as his excuse that "the summer is far spent;" he's to get back to his privateering with no more loss of time or profit. He has no intentions of taking us further up the coast to the Baye of Chesapeake where the Cittie of Ralegh is to be established.

"You'll hang for this," fumes Captain White, but Fernandes merely laughs.

"I'll be well rid of you and the others soon enough!"

"What calumny," mutters Father, pacing the planks and fuming though, in truth, there is nothing he or anyone else can say or do. We're all at the mercy of this unscrupulous brigand and English law as we used to know it, means nothing.

And so we remain on board the Lyon, while our brave Captain White and his men explore Roanoak Island. He tells us later how they headed north to where Ralph Lane's men had built a fort in 1585. Though the earthworks were razed down, the building inside and some nearby houses were still standing. Deer grazed on the overgrown melon vines in and about the structures. Captain White gave orders to his men to clear the tangled brush and set about making repairs. He tells us upon his return that it's his decision to stay at this encampment.

"It will be temporary," he assures us all, "until Fernandes can be persuaded to keep his pledge and continue on with the voyage."

But the best news ever comes when our companion flyboat, under command of Edward Spicer, is suddenly sighted off the starboard bow heading most speedily in our direction. The lookout gives a loud call,

"Ship to the starboard!" and we all rush deckside to

watch its approach.

"Hip-hip-hurrah! Hip-hip-hurrah!" we yell in a rousing cry of joy. Our long-lost escort cuts the waters deep with her prow and the wind carries the voices of her crew and colonists, singing out God's name in praise and thankfulness.

"Simon Fernandes is most distressed at this new turn of events," George smiles.

"Why?"

"He thought it was sunk and gone from mind forever. My father and Master Bayley think he was glad to deal only with some of us, not all."

"How in God's good name did Edward Spicer find us? How did he avoid the Spanish ships?"

"He's an excellent seaman and navigator. It's much to his credit that he was able to retrace the Lyon's path."

I think then of Edward Spicer, lost and alone on the mighty Western Ocean with its turbulent storms, searching the endless horizon day after day for his flagship, the Red Lyon. Surely his prayers and those of our fellow colonists flew swiftly to Heaven, for they were lucky to avoid any Spanish ships, as lucky as we.

In spite of our great anxiety over what is happening between Captain White and Fernandes, we're merry to know that those on the flyboat are, indeed, safe once more.

Chapter 17

Roanoak Island

OH, IT SEEMS THAT WE GO from one calamity to another.
We've disembarked from both the Lyon and the flyboat and
headed inland for the fort. It's to be our new, though temporary, home. John White is still under the assumption that
Fernandes will honor his pledge to sail us further north to the
Chesapeake Baye, but he has made the fort ready for our
arrival.

"This is so exciting," I exclaim to Mother, running
through the dwelling which is to be ours.

"It needs a lot of work," she comments ruefully.

We set up our households, though several of us have to
share until enough timber has been cut to afford new structures. Mother's concern is for Mistress Harvye and sweet
Eleanor. She wants them to share with us. Both Dyonis and
Ananyas decline, saying that it wouldn't be fitting for children
to be in the house where their wives will be birthing.

"I'm not a child," I cry indignantly.

"I know you aren't," Mother says, "but we have Thomas, have you forgotten?"

Indeed, I've forgotten about my younger brother. He's spending a great deal of time with the other boys, while I feel so very close to Mistress Eleanor.

"I would love to stay with you," she confides, and so I run to Mother with her request.

But it's decided, with Ananyas's approval, that I'll move into their dwelling so as to assist her in every way and provide sisterly comfort. I'm overjoyed. It means more freedom for me than I've experienced in a long time for Ananyas, as one of White's assistants, is always by his side these days.

Eleanor and I are able to spend long moments discussing many things which have plagued me, like having babies and knowing when you are or aren't in love.

Mother attends to Mistress Harvye, taking Elizabeth Glande with her on all occasions. That poor goodwife has managed to overcome her grief at her husband's betrayal and is often seen smiling and laughing with the other men around the fort. Mother shakes her head a great deal and sees that Mistress Elizabeth is kept very busy mending and cooking throughout the day.

"Where is George these days?" Eleanor asks me one afternoon as we're busily stitching.

"He's with Father and some of the others, felling trees and learning carpentry."

"Young George is a skilled apprentice," Father comments later that evening. "He has a talent with wood."

"Just like you, dear Arnold," smiles Mother.

We're all eating together, having invited Master Ananyas and Mistress Eleanor to supper. George is there also and it's just like a family celebration. I keep glancing at George and he at me, while his father and mine engage in noisy conversation. Mother and Eleanor are chatting about babies. Thomas is busy whittling a piece of wood in the corner.

"Thomas is making a deer," I say to George.

"I've missed you sorely," he whispers.

"Me also," I whisper back.

"Can you meet me outside in a few moments?"

I barely nod my head, aware that my face must be flush with illicit intent.

So when George gets up to leave, saying he's stiff and wants to stretch his legs, I hastily finish my soup and begin gathering the dishes.

"Shall I take these outside to wash, Mother?"

She gives me just a quick glance since she's so busy in conversation. I can't believe my good fortune. I go out quickly and put the dishes into the pan used for washing. There is George waiting in the twilight.

We have but a fleeting kiss, a moment of holding hands before his father comes out. And the next day, George Howe, the elder, is most savagely murdered.

There have been so many conflicting reports that it's hard to know exactly what happened. These past few days have been such good ones as we clear away the overgrown tangle of brush and structure our new houses. Father says that the trees here are magnificent. They're called loblolly pines, with straight hard trunks and limbs, so perfect for the posts and beams needed for our houses. We've seen no signs of Savages other than our own two, as Father calls them. They willingly pitch in to help, cutting through the tangled vines and sawing branches.

Inside the standing houses, the women clear the cobwebs and begin putting things in order. Outside, the sound of trees crashing is a welcome one. Though we know in our hearts that Chesapeake Baye is where we should be, it appears that Captain White has resigned himself to settling here on Roanoak Island. Perhaps he feels it's a more hospitable place, for Father says he told them all at a meeting that the Heathens of Chesapeake are known to be warlike in their ways. Perhaps he knows in his heart that the rogue, Simon Fernandes, can't be persuaded to continue on this journey.

But of all the horrors, this is surely the worst. George Howe, the elder, had undertaken to wander near the shoreline where he was indulging in crabbing. So intent was he in this endeavor, that a band of hostiles was able to creep upon him alone and defenseless and slay him with arrows. Several of our men found him later but it was too late. George is distraught with the news, for now he's completely alone.

"Oh, George, I'm grieving for you," and I throw my arms about him with no regard to Mother standing there. He clings to me while I hold him sorrowing against my breast. He weeps uncontrollably and I can't do a thing to console him. My tears mingle with his, so Mother sends me back to sit with Eleanor, who weeps, as we all do, for the loss of such a good man.

It's unknown to us whether this attack had been planned, or whether Master Howe had been spotted inadvertently by a group of hostiles hunting for deer. In any event, they escaped back to the mainland while we remain upon Roanoak, shaken to our very foundations.

Chapter 18

Another Tragedy

WHAT AN AIR OF GLOOM PERVADES our encampment now! The men brought back the body of Master Howe and we buried him amidst prayers and tears. The women no longer sing; the men are armed with matchlocks whenever they cut the trees, with at least one who stands at lookout. George remains secluded, though Father and some of the others have tried to persuade him to join them.

"It's no good for young George to be grieving so," Father tells Mother. "We must convince him to shake off this mantle of gloom and put his back into work once more."

"He's young, my dear, and deep in his sorrow. He needs time."

Father just shakes his head and goes back to the timbers. A while later, I ask Mother if I might bring George some food. To my joy, she agrees and helps prepare the meal.

"George has suffered a grievous loss," she sighs, giving me a kiss on the cheek. "We must all be patient with him."

George isn't inclined to eat much, but the smell of Mother's good stew is too much even for him to resist. I watch as he eats, his eyes still red and puffed.

"George," I say with a boldness that amazes me, "it's not good for you to be alone and grieving so. Father thinks you should be back at work. Work helps the heart to heal."

He says nothing but continues eating. Finally he rises, hands me the plate and places his hand under my chin.

"You're... right, sweet Jess," he says with great and painful effort. "My father wouldn't want me to languish here when I can be of use."

I stand there holding the plate awkwardly in my hands while George lays his head upon my shoulder. He gives a great sigh then kisses me softly upon the lips, a sweet and gentle kiss without passion but with much love. I follow him into the sunlight and watch him gather his tools.

"Take care," I call and he waves back. Stay clear of the Savages, I think to myself, as I've steered clear of Manteo and Towaye since this awful incident.

It's true that the Savages have been given a wide berth by most of us, except Captain White and some of the other men. As for me, I don't venture outside when they are about. Father assures me that they're different from the wild hostiles who slew Master Howe, for those have no knowledge of our English ways and our beloved Virgin Queen.

"Manteo speaks our tongue and has bowed before Elizabeth at Court," Father reminds me. "He's a Croatoan whose people are friendly toward strangers."

Captain Stafford has been given orders by John White to take Manteo and several of our colonists to Manteo's home island, there to meet with his people and renew the old friendship. In addition, they hope to learn the fate of Grenville's men before us. Father is going with them, much to Mother's consternation, as are Masters Dyonis and Ananyas. I think it's a bad choice, since Mistress Eleanor is due to give birth in less than three weeks and Mistress Harvye can't be left alone either. Mother has arranged to have both of them move in with us. We are, indeed, a crowded household now.

Upon Father's safe return, we celebrated and made merry. He told us that they sailed to Chacandepeco, as Manteo's tribe calls their village, where the tribe was alarmed at first by their arrival due to the weapons the men carried. But upon Manteo's own words, his people threw aside their bows and arrows and rejoiced in his return.

The fate of the fifteen men left by Richard Grenville in 1586 has now been determined. They foolishly placed no guard and were attacked by a marauding band of hostiles belonging to the tribe of Wingina. Two were killed and the remaining thirteen escaped. Father said that Manteo's people didn't know where they were.

John White fumes inwardly, pacing back and forth before his dwelling. Father says he's deciding what to do about the attack on George's father. And he hasn't forgotten Simon Fernandes, that pirate who still commandeers the Lyon, anchored just beyond Roanoak Island.

"It's a heavy load for one man to carry," comments Father and this is true, indeed. I'm glad to be a young woman, without such heavy weight upon my shoulders. I even gave Thomas a kiss last night before he went to bed, which made him quite puzzled. Then he wiped my kiss off his cheek and stuck his tongue out at me behind Father's back.

On August ninth, early in the morning, John White and Edward Stafford, along with twenty-four others and Manteo, laid seige to the village of Dasamonquepeuc at the far end of

Roanoak. There they attacked some hostiles without warning as a punishment for the murder of Master Howe.

They killed one and routed the others. Alas, it was a terrible tragedy compounded upon the first, for these weren't the hostiles who had slain George's father, but those of Manteo's own tribe who'd come from Croatoan Island to gather corn and fruit.

"Manteo broods most sorely," Father says, grimly shaking his head. "For surely he knew his own people and yet allowed the attack to continue."

I can't fathom the heart of this Savage who moves about our settlement like one possessed. I'm sore afraid. Even the men now stay clear of his path as he struts from one place to another, Towaye always following. He's an imposing figure, this dark-skinned Savage with his black piercing eyes. My dreams have returned to plague me and I toss and turn each night. Mother thinks I'm coming down with the ague and plies me with hot tea and Mistress Steueens's sweet honey.

He isn't even handsome as I deem a man handsome, like George or my Father. He wears his hair long on the sides and pulled back to be fastened loosely at the neck. The hair on top of his head is short-cropped and stands straight up. He has many ornaments of shell and copper, and a strange tattoo adorns his shoulder. He's neither young nor old and moves like a cat upon silent feet. I've strange feelings whenever I see him near, turning to avoid his presence. He fills me with dread, yet an odd exhilaration. In my dreams there is always a figure in shadow dressed like he, yet not of substance. This ghost sweeps me into his arms and carries me away. I don't know my destination but I'm not afraid. I want this apparition to be George, who has kissed and held me, but I know it's not. Oh, how may I be rid of these strange and unknown feelings?

Chapter 19

A New Daughter

"BY THE COMMANDMENT OF SIR WALTER RALEGH, thus do I baptize and give unto you the title 'Lord of Roanoak thereof, and Dasamonquepeuc, in reward of your faithful service.'"

And so Manteo is annointed with Holy Water and baptized into Christian doctrine, a ceremony led by Roger Prat before us all on this day of our Lord, August thirteenth, 1587.

Father explains that this ceremony has been Sir Walter's intent, in letters written and handed over to our captain by George Carey on the Isle of Wight. It's a laying aside of all ill feeling and a cementing of the bond between our colonists and the Croatoan people.

"It's a moving forward out of darkness, bringing the light of our Good Lord to the savages. Surely you must believe this is a worthy undertaking, Jess."

I just stand there watching and not understanding it all. Manteo carries himself proudly before our colonists, while

Master Prat reads passages from Tyndale's Bible and blesses the water before he uses it to mark a cross on the Savage's forehead. Thomas is pulling on my hand, no doubt bored beyond tears and wanting nothing more than to play with the other boys.

"Stop," I admonish him though I, too, am getting tired of standing. I can't hear all the words spoken and the afternoon is growing hotter. Margaret Harvye and Eleanor aren't in attendance and for a moment, I envy them.

I confess, I'm glad when George reaches for my hand and gives it a quick squeeze. I pay scant attention after that to what's going on before me.

George has been taken under wing by Father. This means I see more of him than before, which makes me glad. He's always asking questions and our conversations around the supper table have become more lively and challenging.

"Why did Sir Walter instruct Captain White in Manteo's baptism?"

"To establish him in a Christian manner as lord over his own people."

"Master Bayley said it was to hold fast to this territory while we were in Chesapeake," George adds.

"That's correct."

"But sir, why does Simon Fernandes still wait aboard the Lyon?"

"Yes, Father," I eagerly interrupt, "that scoundrel still sits at anchor. I thought he was anxious to sail?"

"John White also puzzles over that," remarks Father, scratching his head, "as do we all."

I sit at the table and watch Father and George engage in such conversation. There is life coming back into George's eyes and I know my father is growing fond of him. This pleases me immensely.

Five days after Manteo's baptism, I am called to Mother's side to assist Eleanor Dare in her birthing.

"Bring hot water and towels," Mother calls to me. "And ask Mistress Steueens to come quickly, if it pleases her."

"Oh, oh, I can't...!" Eleanor cries out. She is straining and suffering badly, her pains coming every two minutes.

"What can I do?" Ananyas is at his wit's end, pacing back and forth, the sweat rising on his forehead.

"You must leave us," says Mother firmly and pushes Ananyas toward the door. "Go now and ask God's blessing for your wife."

Mistress Steueens hurries in with basins for the hot water and clean cloths for the newborn babe. Eleanor has prepared infant clothes which she must have carried with her all the way from England. I've never seen anything so small and dainty.

Mistress Steueens wants to send me from the room but Mother insists that I stay.

"She's too young," Mistress Steueens keeps saying over and over. Mother shakes her head.

"She's a grown woman now," and I could have fairly kissed her.

"Ananyas, Ananyas!" Eleanor keeps calling, tossing and turning in her labors. Mother wipes the sweat from her, while I hold her hand and Mistress Steueens hovers near. My poor hand is slowly being crushed just like Mother's had been with Mistress Harvye in her false labor, but I hardly notice. Poor sweet Eleanor, I think, if this is what a woman must go through to bring life into the world, I wonder if it's worth the suffering.

Mother is quite worried because she labors so long, having begun her pains the evening before. She tells Mistress

Steueens that the child is of good size and Eleanor's hips too small. Though I've learned somewhat about how babies begin, all my questions about how they are birthed are suddenly answered when Eleanor gives one long, wrenching scream and the babe's head is seen.

"Oh, what joy!" smiles Mother. "Come, Jess, and see new life in the making."

I confess, I don't find it glorious as she claims, but rather messy and disgusting.

"Push, push," encourages Mother and so, Eleanor pushes and pushes and soon the whole body slips out. Mistress Steueens cuts the cord with a large knife that has been boiled in water. Then she takes the infant girl and cleans her, wrapping her in a blanket.

"Pray give her to me," whispers Eleanor weakly, and the babe is laid in her arms. Mother changes the birthing sheets for clean ones, sponges Eleanor and brushes her hair. Only then is Ananyas allowed to come in.

"You have a new daughter," Mother whispers, tears in her eyes. Then she shoos me out along with herself and Mistress Steueens, leaving him alone with his wife and his new child.

Chapter 20

"A Fair Child"

ELEANOR, FOR SHE SAYS I MAY CALL HER by her given name, lets me hold her new-born babe. I confess, I'm afraid I might drop it, so tiny and fragile it seems.

The little one is sleeping when put in my arms, but she opens her eyes to stare at me. Then she gives a yawn and goes back to sleep. I sit next to the bed holding her, while Mother fusses with the bedclothes. Eleanor looks pale and tired but whenever she sees her child, her eyes fairly light up.

"What a little creature," I say, playing with the tiny fingers.

"Just like your doll," Mother comments.

"Oh, Mother, I haven't played with her for years."

"Better than a doll," Eleanor smiles, then makes a face. "Except when she cries. Come, give her to me, it's almost time for her feeding."

I'm so embarrassed when Eleanor pulls her garment to one side and puts the babe to her breast. My face reddens and

I drop my eyes.

"Why, Jess, it's a natural thing to suckle a babe," smiles Eleanor. "One day when you're married, you'll have your own."

Mother gives a smile and I blush again, for whom will I marry? That hasn't been discussed, though I hope it might be George. I try to imagine myself as Mistress Howe, keeping a household with small children tugging on my skirts.

"Not for a while," says Mother softly, reading my mind. "Come now and help me with the cooking."

So we leave Eleanor and her new-born child. Ananyas and John White, her father, are coming up the path from the woodlands.

"Oh, Ananyas," I call out. "It's a pretty babe, indeed, most fair and so tiny."

He laughs and strides on past. John White stops for a moment and speaks.

"A fair child, my granddaughter? Then I'm most pleased. Are you helping to take care of her?"

I redden once more.

"Just a little. Mother does most of the caring."

I skip back to where Mother is busy making a stew.

"He's so nice," I say, my words all in a rush.

"Ananyas?"

"He, too. No, I meant Captain White. He was kind when he showed us around the Lyon, and kinder now when he spoke of his grandchild."

"For a man to live to see his grandchild is a remarkable thing," says Mother. She closes her eyes. "Perhaps your father and I will be so fortunate...."

Then she realizes what she's said.

"We have time," she laughs. "You're young yet."

"But grown to womanhood already."

"That's true."

"Mother, how old were you when you married Father? And when you had me?"

"Why, I was seventeen," she replies, blushing. "And eighteen when I gave birth, a year younger than Mistress Eleanor." Then she sends me for more water.

So, I think, I have three more years. A great deal can happen in that time. George might fall out of love with me, or I with him. Oh, how can I wait so long?

The days pass quickly and before we know it, the occasion of the babe's christening is upon us. Oh, what a joy and celebration it is! In honor of our beloved Virgin Queen and the land we've settled, Ananyas and Eleanor name her Virginia. Father says she's the first babe to be born in these western parts. It's a good omen for our new world and we all make merry.

George grows more daring. When he thinks no one is looking, he reaches out and touches my hand. Once, his fingers curled around mine. We stole a fleeting kiss behind the supply house, then walked in opposite directions for fear someone was watching. His eyes still hold a deep sadness, for the loss of his father will never be forgotten. George Howe, the elder, was a good man, raising George from boyhood after his wife died in her second childbirthing, along with the babe.

I see little of Manteo and Towaye these days, and give thanks that they're busy with the others, preparing the Lyon and the flyboat for departure back to England. I go about my daily responsibilites with a quick step and spend a great deal of time with sweet Eleanor and her little Virginia.

Chapter 21

Thoughts Of England

WE'RE ALL WRITING LETTERS to send back to England with the Lyon. It's a time of great sadness to know that the link with our beloved homeland will soon be broken. Many of the women make tokens to send to relatives back home. Mother asks if I have enough paper to write some letters to my friends, Alice and Mary.

"It would be lovely for them to get your letters. I know you spend a great deal of time writing down your thoughts."

I blush. "Oh, Mother, what shall I say?"

"You can tell them all about the babe, Virginia. You can write how you must feel in this brave, new land. Surely you'll have a great deal to write about."

And so, I sit down to compose my thoughts. I'm not sure what I'll say. I can describe our life here so far, the re-building of the houses, the chores which must be done that I'd never have undertaken at home: fetching water, tending to Eleanor and her babe. I might even try to tell them what the sea voyage was like, but it will be hard to write about all that in such a short letter.

Or I can write about George, his father's death and my feelings for him. That should be an easy task. Mary and Alice will surely be envious of his attentions to me though by now, I'm certain, they have young men swooning over them. I sorely miss other girls my age, even though Eleanor has certainly been a good confidante.

Should I write about the strange Manteo and how he comes and goes, slipping through our encampment, sometimes aloof, sometimes toiling side by side with the men as they prepare the boats for sailing? Should I tell of my feelings whenever I see him? I'm not sure what I feel, a certain quickening of the blood, a start of breath held, then released. It's not the strange stirrings inside whenever I see George, that longing of my youth, as Eleanor describes it, to be a woman loved and cherished.

Should I tell of how I think he sometimes watches me, though it must surely be my imagination? These are thoughts I can never reveal to another. One thing I know for certain. I can have no bond with any Savage in this wild and untamed land.

The letter has to be put aside, for in the middle of writing, Mistress Harvye suddenly goes into labor. It's unlike Eleanor's labor in which she strained and suffered for so long. Mistress Harvye's babe is born within two hours of her final confinement. Mother says it's because she's already birthed one child, Agnes, so things go smoothly. I can hear her cries though, and go to sit with Eleanor throughout the ordeal.

"Why is it that women suffer so much pain?"

"It's God's will," Eleanor replies calmly. "Eve labored to bring forth Cain and Abel. It's written in our Holy Bible that man is wrought of pain and suffering."

"I think I'll have no children," I say firmly.

Eleanor laughs. "You'll change your mind once you have a husband."

I shake my head. "Let him have the babies then."

Eleanor laughs out loud. "Silly goose," she gives me a quick kiss. "Men cannot have babies. They're not built for it."

"Mother said you labored so long because it was your first."

"It's true. The first time is often hard for women. Once the second and third ones come, the passage is easy into this world."

"If I have a difficult time, then I'll have only one child."

She laughs again. "First none, then one. Make up your mind, Jess."

Mistress Harvye has a boy child. Dyonis is beside himself with joy. The babe is black-haired and red-faced, bigger than little Virginia. They name him Christopher Walter Ralegh. Dyonis gets drunk on spirits and has to be put to bed by Father and some of the others. Mother cries when she sees the babe.

"Now we have two new little colonists," she says through her tears.

We're close to the time of departure for the Lyon and the flyboat. The men have spent many hours washing down the holds with vinegar to remove the smells and accumulations. Father says the ships are being newly calked in preparation for the heavy seas. Sweet water and wood have been loaded on. Father and the others beg John White's assistants to pick two of their own to return to England with Fernandes, who anchors still off shore. The men are afraid we'll be forgotten and that no one will return with supplies for us. Philip of Spain was rumored to be building his Armada even as we left Portsmouth. Father says we need agents in London to see that Elizabeth doesn't forget us in her troubles with the Spaniards.

At first, Ananyas says he will go, but Father and Roger Prat won't hear of it.

"Your place is with your wife and newborn child," they say in one voice. "And we have need of your talents as a brick maker." So brave Ananyas agrees to remain.

The assistants and John White have met several times and there's bitter discussion. I don't know what's being said, but Father paces the floor and waits for word. I'm glad my father isn't one of the assistants, after all, for theirs is an unhappy lot, to choose who must return. Father's skills as a carpenter are sorely needed here and so, he and Ananyas will stay along with Dyonis, who is also newly a father.

Then Father tells us that Christopher Cooper has agreed to go, as he's unmarried and a good speaker for our cause. There's great relief, though Father says that the men still want two agents on our behalf, each with powers of persuasion that will match the Queen's determination to confront King Philip. But later this evening, Christopher Cooper withdraws his willingness to set sail, so now the colonists are pleading for Captain White himself to return. Father says he is, in truth, the only one who knows our situation here in Roanoak and will be most eloquent on our behalf.

We had no sleep last night, for the men of our encampment were up and the air rang with loud discussion. John White isn't disposed to pack up and leave us "abandoned," as he calls it. According to Father, he still feels we'll move eventually to a proper settlement of the Cittie of Ralegh in the Baye of Chesapeake.

"We've given him a proposition in writing," Father explains, "of our intentions that he be our representative with Elizabeth. Master Sampson drew it up since he has the power of attorney at his disposal."

"What does it say, Arnold?"

"That we authorize him to act as agent with our full knowledge and consent, on our behalf; to gather supplies once he reaches London; then to set sail and return to Roanoak with such provisions as will last us until we settle in Chesapeake."

Father smiles. "It's all very eloquent and serious as befits such a document. But its meaning is clear. We honor the possessions that he leaves behind and promise guardianship of his family."

"Oh, Arnold," gasps Mother, clutching her hand to her breast. "And he with a new granddaughter. How will he bear it!"

Chapter 22

A Letter Home

DEAR MARY AND ALICE,

I'm writing this letter to both of you though I know you'll probably never read it. Last night at midnight, Captain John White boarded a small boat to sail to the outer waters where the flyboat and the Lyon were anchored. I wasn't sorry to see Simon Fernandes leave these shores, but Captain White's absence will be sorely felt.

Captain White bade fond adieu to his daughter Eleanor, Ananyas and his new-born granddaughter, Virginia. It was a sad moment for all. Sweet Eleanor was in tears, though she tried so hard to be brave. Father and daughter embraced for a long time. It was like an arrow in the heart to see our captain gently kiss the cheek of the babe. He and Ananyas shook hands, clasping each other tightly. Then he grasped the hand of each man remaining. Most of the women wept, including my dear mother, though she insisted there was something in her eye.

"Goodbye," he called. "Goodbye to all of you, my dear friends."

He spoke words of inspiration and courage to each and every family. He clapped George on the back and bade him turn his attentions to the future, not the past. Then, to my great surprise, he leaned over and kissed my cheek. I must have blushed because everyone began to laugh.

The Lyon, which has ridden anchor beyond the inlet for the month we've been here, heaved to and set broad sail for England. The companion flyboat, with John White on board, sailed just behind. The weather now is favorable though just a few days earlier, a mighty storm had approached from the south bringing heavy rains and high winds. It caused Fernandes to cut his cables and head toward deeper waters. We thought for certain he wouldn't return. Father's wondered many a time why he waited off shore all these days, when surely he could have sailed away, "to seek plunder," as he so fervently wished to do. Father said it's a mystery whose answer we may never know.

A heavy heart weighs upon us all, for John White was not only our leader but our inspiration. It was he who led the way to this new world and under his guidance, we were to establish the Cittie of Ralegh and build a new life. Now he's set sail for England and left us behind, without benefit of his experience and wisdom.

"Still," says Father with a smile, "he's left a company of brave men and women who'll carve out the wilderness and shape it to their liking."

I can see that Mother isn't completely convinced, though she does her best to hide it from both me and Thomas. She busies herself about the house, cleaning, cooking and visiting Eleanor and Margaret Harvye almost every day. Most often,

I accompany her to assist with the babes, holding them and changing them when necessary. I tell you, dear Mary and Alice, that I've become quite the expert at swaddling a babe and singing to it.

Eleanor grows stronger every day, as does Mistress Margaret. They both smile a lot, even though a veiled sadness haunts Eleanor's eyes. Like George, she grieves quietly for the loss of her father.

Little Christopher Walter Ralegh Harvye was christened. The ceremony was a quiet one compared to the merriment of the first baptism. There never was a prouder man than Dyonis, holding his infant son while the Holy Waters were poured upon his head. What a scream came from the mouth of that tiny babe! We all laughed. In a moment of boldness, I asked Eleanor how Ananyas felt about having a daughter rather than a son.

"How should he feel?" she asked in return, giving me a strange look.

"I don't know," I answered. "I see how Dyonis rejoices in his son. Is it true that men prefer sons to daughters?"

"Indeed, I doubt it," she said quickly. "Ananyas told me it was of no consequence that we had a girl first." She paused. "There'll be other babes and, perhaps, many sons."

I let the matter drop, but when I mentioned it later to Mother, she chastised me for asking.

"A healthy babe is all that men and women should wish for, nothing more or less."

Now I feel badly and want to make it up to Eleanor by playing more with little Virginia. Indeed, when I watch Ananyas with his daughter, I can hardly see the difference between him and Dyonis. So if men want sons instead of daughters, it's their business and no one else's.

Tonight we'll hold a prayer meeting for the safe journey of John White to England, the favor of our beloved Queen to shine upon us all and his most speedy return to these far shores.

Respectfully yours,

Jessabel Archarde

Chapter 23

The Bear Hunt

THERE'S BEEN MUCH TO DO in the time since John White's departure. First, the men appointed Roger Prat as leader.

"He's a good man," says Father. "He can devote all his time and energies to our well-being and safety."

Before he left, Captain White pledged Manteo's and Towaye's allegiance to those of us remaining. Ananyas told us of the ceremony.

"For their benefit, our captain made them swear upon the Holy Bible and recite an oath. This they did willingly, for Manteo takes his Christian baptism seriously. He bade them stay within our encampment and not return to their tribe."

Father and Ananyas discuss the wisdom of this, for Manteo will still act as translator and it's hoped the others of Manteo's tribe will share their food with us during the difficult winter which lies ahead.

Ananyas also tells us that John White has instructed us

all to leave a sign, should we move on toward Chesapeake Baye.

"It's to be a carving upon a doorpost or a tree of the name where we move, so when he returns it shall be easier to find us. And if we're distressed, we're to carve a cross upon the letters, plain for him to see."

At this, Mother put a finger to her lips but it's too late. We all hear Ananyas's words, Thomas, myself and Eleanor. I go to sleep that night haunted once again by my old dreams and a new one, of being attacked and fire arrows sailing in our midst.

And today, our brave men announce they're going on a bear hunt. One was seen just yesterday on the outskirts of our encampment where the trees begin to grow thick and close together. George told me he even saw its large brownish shape looming behind the brushline. He could hear it snuffling and snorting. It's the first bear to be seen nearby, though Father says that the men have reported seeing some further north as they hunt for small game and deer.

"You must be careful," I caution George. "Bears can be very dangerous."

"I have my matchlock," he replies, straightening up his back and shouldering the musket. How much like his father he looks. "We'll have all the men for protection."

"I know that Father's going with you, though Mother would much prefer he stay here."

George leans over and gives me a quick kiss on my cheek. Oh, how brazen we're becoming, to kiss thus without a thought as to who might be watching. I don't even glance around to see if we're alone but, liking his boldness, turn my cheek in readiness for his affection.

"You must stay close to the houses," he cautions then.

86

"Who knows which direction the animal may take. He could come charging right through here."

I give a shudder, imagining the great furred bear lumbering straight toward me, snuffling and baring its teeth. When he turns to go, I grab his arm.

"Come back safely," and I watch as he and Father join the other men. Aware of his warning, I gather Agnes and some of the smaller boys and take them inside to play a game.

This evening we hear loud triumphant cries as the men come back to camp, the huge brown bear strung on poles which they strain to carry. Everyone runs out to greet them.

"Come, come, they're back. Oh, see what they've got. Come quickly, everyone!"

The young boys fairly trip them up, they're so anxious to see the fearsome animal up close. I take Agnes's hand and approach, watching them anchor the poles in tall wooden sprockets, leaving the animal for all to admire.

"Oh, it smells," says Agnes, wrinkling up her nose. In truth, it does smell quite strongly, a sour odor of earth, scorched fur and blood. When I look closely, I can see the blood still smearing its sides, the froth upon its mouth, its eyes dull in death.

"Come away," I say, pulling Agnes's hand. "This isn't a pretty sight for you to see."

"I want to stay," she answers petulantly, stamping her foot. So we linger a while longer. Even Mother comes to see what all the commotion is about. The women gather in small groups.

"What's so special about a bear?" Agnes asks me. Mistress Steueens replies.

"It means food for us through the chilly Autumn months and oil for our candle wicks."

Thomas and the other boys keep touching it and hanging on every word the men speak. They run back and forth between the men and the bear so as not to miss a thing.

"It was so exciting, Jess. We tracked the bear for many hours. What a difficult time we had. The trail wound up and down and we were so footsore. With darkness approaching, we started to make a small camp for the night. But out of the blackness we saw its eyes, like yellow spots. So we crept away from the fire and flushed it out. It came at us with a roar, its tongue hanging out, snarling and growling. We shot, it stumbled but then got up again and charged once more."

"Oh, George," I gasp. "What did you do?"

"I wanted to run," he laughs, "but I didn't...."

"... It was Manteo's arrow which brought it down," says Ananyas, wiping the sweat and streaks of dirt from his brow. "While we fumbled with our powder and match, he shot it straight through the heart."

"It fell right at my feet," says George. "I confess, I was about to turn and run when it dropped just a few feet away."

I glance at the creature hanging so ignobly in death. It's then I see the feathered arrow still protruding from its chest, the fur blackened and burned around the wound. A strange shudder catches my limbs and I can't stop from trembling. Mother sees me thus and sends us back, Agnes to Mistress Harvye and me to our house.

I leave the sounds of riotous celebration behind, lie down on my bed and draw the covers up around me. Before my closed eyes I see the bear charging, the bow drawn back in a mighty pull, the fire arrow speeding swiftly through the air, the dark-skinned Savage gleaming silver in the moonlight.... Then an all-encompassing blackness envelopes me and I know no more.

Chapter 24

Shorter Days

FOR TWO DAYS, OUR LIVES CENTER around the bear. The men skin it, a messy affair which I refuse to watch, though Thomas does so with great glee. They cut off its head and stick it on a pole at the farthest end of the encampment. I don't venture in that direction, nor do I let Agnes go.

The women who know how render the fat into oil for our lamps and wicks. Each family is given a portion of the meat. There's so much of it, we're overflowing with food. We hold a community feast the next day, with dancing and story telling. I must confess that I find bear meat truly delicious, succulent and rich. It's a rare treat to feast so indulgently.

Manteo receives much praise for killing the bear. In their panic at seeing so large an animal up close, the men had merely wounded it. There might have been serious damage done if the fire arrow hadn't found its mark so accurately. The men make a point of congratulating him many times, even those who didn't go on the hunt. It seems he's highly pleased with all the attention and is even seen smiling. Strange, but I never thought a Savage could smile.

Father's been telling us of the stories Manteo has told about his tribe, his children. He speaks not of his wife and Father wonders if she's dead these many years. I confess I never thought of Manteo as a husband and a father before. I wonder how many sons and daughters he may have, if they're young like Agnes or older like me and George. When I ask Father his age, he replies,

"Manteo tells me he has seen many winters. That's the Indian way to speak of the passing of years. My guess is that he's older than I in age."

"How can that be?" I answer boldly, then lower my face in shame. Father laughs.

"Do I look older because of my beard?" He ruffles my hair. "Silly goose, Jess. I'm not yet an old man, only thirty-eight." He and Mother exchange a look and both begin laughing out loud. I'm so embarrassed and don't look my father in the eye for the rest of the day.

Now Manteo struts about the camp with triumphant airs, Towaye always close by. Why does it annoy me so?

"He's reveling in his glorious accomplishment," I complain to George.

"Why not?" George gives a shrug of his shoulders. "He saved us all. Without his fire arrow, Jess, some of us would have been badly injured or even killed. It takes time to fire a musket and an angry bear is nothing to tangle with."

"Why does he have to parade in such a manner?"

George stares at me.

"He's a warrior, a hunter for his people, surely something of which to be proud."

He stares again, quizzically.

91

"And why should it bother you, my dear Jess. He's nothing to us."

George pulls me then behind the nearest tree and begins kissing me in a most passionate manner. I can't get my breath and push him away.

"Oh, let me breathe, I'm suffocating!"

And step back to see Manteo standing ten paces away, watching us.

"Oh," I gasp. George grabs my hand, nods curtly to the Savage and we both run back to the houses, though I glance back several times to see him standing there, staring after us.

And still there's no word of Captain White and his voyage home.

"We'll not hear for many weeks, even months," says Father. "The voyage itself will take a long time, then there's the audience with our Queen, then he must gather monies for more men and supplies. After that, he must provision the ships and, finally, there's the long navigation across the sea once more to where we are. You must learn patience, Jess," he adds. "Such things aren't accomplished hurridly. In the meanwhile, we must provide for the approaching winter."

There's little to harvest, since we haven't been here long enough to plant crops. Instead, we gather wild beans, which Manteo calls *okindgier*, onions, carrots and some melon fruits called *macocqwer*. The people of his tribe come once again to Roanoak from their Croatoan Island to offer us maize, a yellow vegetable which tastes delicious when roasted over a fire. Its Indian name is *pagatowr*. They also show us how to grind it down into flour for baking. Roger Prat organizes the men into many different hunting and gathering groups. Whatever small game is caught is smoked for later use. There's a great debate over whether we should stay here and try to survive the winter, or gather ourselves together to make our own way toward the Baye of Chesapeake.

The nights have begun to grow colder and daylight hours are shorter, for it's already the twentieth day of September. Father, George, Ananyas, Dyonis and some of the others decide to organize a fishing expedition to the coast. They expect to gather many fish, which will surely supplement our supplies. I beg to go with them, having been left behind on other forages, but Father's adamant.

"This isn't woman's work," he says firmly. "You'll stay home and help Mistresses Eleanor and Margaret with their babes. And your mother," he adds. Then he gives me an unexpected kiss. "We'll not be gone that long."

But Mother's terribly afraid they'll stumble upon the same hostiles who slew George's father. So Manteo and Towaye have been chosen to go along as guides and protectors. Once more I sit, chafing under the role I have to play. I am guardian to the younger children, nurse to the babies, and unable to explore or see this new land for myself. Only the confines of the settlement are allowed. I'm not allowed to venture beyond the cleared places; the ring of pines is to be my boundary. Mother knows I'm upset by this. She tries to keep me busy and involved in what she's doing.

And so I make the best of it, playing with the babes when they're awake, holding long discussions with Eleanor, teaching Agnes how to read and write her letters, writing my thoughts down on my precious sheets of paper. One day, perhaps, this will make an interesting story for my children and grandchildren to read.

Chapter 25

The Accident

WE HEAR HIM SCREAMING LONG BEFORE the men bring him back to the settlement.

"What a terrible accident," cries Master Spendlove. "He didn't have a chance."

"Who is it?" exclaims Elizabeth Viccars.

"John Tydway," we're told. "He was accidentally pinned by a falling tree. Though he saw it crashing, he couldn't move fast enough. The tree caught his legs and crushed both of them."

"Jess, fetch me some hot water and some clean cloths. Hurry!"

Mother shoos the younger boys away and rushes with some of the other women to his aid. The doctor is summoned, a strange man as I've come to know him, full of incantations and woefully short on knowledge.

"Hmm, let me see," he says, poking and prodding Master Tydway's broken bones, which causes the poor man to scream even louder. Then he just shakes his head and says,

"No use, no use. There's too much damage."

Mistresses Steueens and Viccars hurry him away. Mother washes the torn skin of its blood and dirt. In truth, there's nothing to be done. The bones protrude through his legs from the terrible break. Oh, how he screams and sobs. I can't bear it. Mistress Steueens brews him a potion which makes him drift off into a deep drugged sleep, through which he still moans and gnashes his teeth in pain.

By late evening, he's flush with the fever and crying out in delirium. Mother says it's lucky he has neither wife nor child to witness his anguish.

"I shall stay with him all night," she states and does just that, wiping his brow with cool cloths and holding his hand. But by morning, he's dead from the pain and torment.

"A mercy, his heart couldn't take it," my dear mother whispers, her cheeks tear-stained like the rest of us.

"This is a solemn and terrible day," Roger Prat intones, while the women wrap him in soft cloth and the men dig a deep hole beyond the trees. We hold a Christian ceremony and bury him midst tears and great sorrow. A cross is placed to mark his grave.

"...for earth thou art, and unto earth shalt thou return," whispers Master Prat. "The loss of one is the loss of us all." As our minister, he reads many passages from the Holy Bible, though the words give little comfort. Both Eleanor and Margaret Harvye clutch their babes to their breasts, rocking back and forth and humming sweet sad lullabyes. Oh, it's a time of great misery.

This accident has left my dearest mother bereft of laughter. She moves and performs her daily tasks with lips set in a thin line, Frequently, I catch her shoulders heaving in a silent

sob. When at last I hold out my arms to her, she comes to me gladly, leaning her head against my breast. She begins to cry deeply. I hold her close; I, the mother; she, the child, while she clings to me and gives way to her grief. I try to think of some comforting words.

"Hush, hush," I whisper. "Dearest Mother, hush."

How strange to feel such bonding between my mother and me. I hold her as another woman might, a friend to whom she can turn. I hold her as she shakes with sobs, her eyes tear-streaked and swollen, as I held George when his father died. Leaning my cheek against her hair, I stroke its softness and whisper what I know of solace. Then I kiss her hair, her cheek, over and over as she's done to me so many times in my childhood.

"Hush," I whisper. "Hush, it will be all right. You'll see. Soon Father will be home. It will be all right."

"We're so vulnerable," is all she keeps repeating between her sobs. "Strangers in this wild, inhospitable land. Perhaps we never should have left our beloved England."

The men walk around the encampment with dark and somber faces. No one sings now. We wait, instead, for the men of the fishing expedition to return with the greatest of speed. This death has pierced our very hearts.

Chapter 26

A Camp Divided

THE MEN RETURN, LOADED DOWN with fish of all sizes and shapes, and reeking of oils. We hear them singing long before we see them. Roger Prat and a few others go forth to meet them. The singing soon stops and they stride into camp, place their catch on the ground and gather in groups.

"Tell us how it happened?" Father asks.

"There was no hope. We called to him but he couldn't move in time. The tree fell and crushed his legs."

"Thank the good Lord he wasn't married," cries Mistress Viccars. "Or there'd be a widow and young ones to care for."

"Where's Eleanor and the babe?" Ananyas calls.

"Safe."

"I must go see them."

"And I, to see Joyce," adds Father.

He takes Mother in his arms and whispers words that I'm not privy to. Then he kisses her and goes outside, to gather the men together in a big council meeting. It lasts well into the evening. During this time, the women take it upon themselves to clean all the fish and for this, I'm included. Oh, what a messy, smelly job it is to take a knife and scale a fish. They stare at me with their dead bulging eyes while I try not to look. Several times the knife slips and almost cuts me. Then Mistress Powell shows me how to scale the proper way, scraping the knife away from me, after which we cut off the heads and tails, gutting them swiftly and throwing them into buckets of cold water. By the time I'm done, I stink of fish.

"Oh, Mother, I must bathe."

"You can't leave the camp now, 'tis night. Take this lye soap and scrub yourself down."

She hands me the strong pungent soap which smells almost as bad as the fish. I go behind our house where it's more private and scrub my hands and arms til they're raw. Mother joins me after she and the other women have hung the fish. They string them on lines over a smokey fire to cure them. All night long those fires burn, the thick smoke from the green wood curling low in the trees.

Father comes in later and I can hear him whispering to Mother. He tells her how successful the expedition has been. Not only fish were caught, but stone crabs, oysters and cockles as well. He says they saw some hostiles, but they were far away and Manteo warned them in plenty of time. They crouched low in the reeds where they were crabbing, and kept the boats from sailing until the hostiles disappeared.

"It was a good expedition in spite of that," Father says. "But this death at camp has brought great dissent. Some of the men are talking about moving to the Chesapeake, where there are more fortifications."

"He wasn't killed by a hostile," Mother replies. "It was a terrible accident. Must we then pack up?" I can hear the tremor in her voice.

"No one has decided yet what he'll do. I, myself, don't know if we should make such a move. Whatever you do," he cautions, "say nothing to the children."

But I've heard and lie in my bed trembling and fearful.

"I love you madly, Jess," whispers George the next day. "I can't think of my life without you near. Say that you'll stay with me."

"What do you mean? Where are you going, George?"

"Some of the colonists want to search out the Chesapeake and plan to settle there. Others want to stay here and brave the winter's snow. The camp's divided. Can't you hear all the talking?"

And so it's true, what Father first whispered to Mother. Today, we hear nothing but dissension and voices of the men raised in anger. Mother makes me stay inside with Agnes and Eleanor. I've seen nothing of Margaret Harvye and little Christopher. The men stride about the grounds or else, gather in small groups discussing wildly. The camp seems split, Father reports. There are those who wish to take the pinnace, our only boat now, and sail through the inlet and out to the deep waters. Then they'll head north toward the Baye of Chesapeake. The others want to make a permanent settlement here on Roanoak, befriending Manteo's tribe of Croatoans and learning their ways until such time as Captain White returns.

"In truth, George, I don't know which way Mother and Father feel. What do you think?"

"I put my lot in with those who plan to sail north. The winter's coming and we must set sail before ice and snow blind our path."

He grabs my hand.

"Say you'll come wherever I go, sweet Jess. You know

that Captain White didn't plan for us to remain here permanently. It was only because Fernandes refused to continue on his way that we didn't reach our intended destination."

"I can't leave my mother and father, nor Thomas. How can I answer you when I don't know what they plan?"

"Oh, Jess," he sighs, pressing my hand to his lips. "You must ask them and find out. The men who want to leave grow restless and impatient."

I pull away from George's grasp. Surely our encampment can't be split thus. There's safety in numbers only. That's what John White had instructed us; that's what Roger Prat had said when he spoke of Master Tydway's loss as a loss for us all. I see George's face and read his anxiety, but I don't feel like staying near. Instead, I run to search for Father and some answers.

Chapter 27

A New Language

IN TRUTH, THE WINTER IN THIS NEW land will be harsh and difficult. A fierce wind blew up last night, tearing the leaves from the trees and swirling them down. It's the first week of October and the air has turned brisk and cold.

"A hard winter... is coming," Manteo confers with Towaye. "The leaves fall early."

He waves his hands in a large circle. "Snow, *acaunque*, approaches... from the north."

Towaye grunts and speaks to Manteo in their language. It has often puzzled me how Manteo can speak the Queen's English, though haltingly, but not Towaye. Father says he doesn't have the inclination to learn. Unknown to both Father and Mother, I've already mastered some phrases of the Indians, as George now calls them.

"They're not the ones responsible for my father's death," sighs George, a sorrowing look upon his face. "Those came from the northlands across the sound. We must no longer speak of Manteo's tribe as Savages, Jess. If we shouldn't yet leave for Chesapeake and they're to help us survive this winter, we must treat them as fellow beings."

"Then teach me to understand what they're saying. Will you help me speak in their language?"

"I'll do my best. Manteo has been instructing me."

"How does he do it?"

"He begins by pointing to a thing, say a tree, and tells me its name. Then I repeat the sound over and over again until I've learned it well."

"And what's the name for a tree?"

So George has begun teaching me all that he knows. There's so much to learn, my head fairly spins. We walk around the encampment and he points out things, saying the Indian word for them. The tongue is strange, with many different sounds and blends all difficult to pronounce. The word for Indian can be said many different ways: *unqua*, or *nuppin*, or *yauh-he*, depending on the tribe to which one belongs. It's the same for other words. An Englishman can be a *nickreruroh*, or *tosh shonte*, or *wintsohore*, each according to its tribal origin. This island that we've made our home is called *Nauhhoureot*.

I've learned that milkweed in Croatoan is called *wysauke* and *wapeih* is clay. George makes me repeat the words again and again. He's even begun teaching me easy phrases such as, "*Unta hah*," for "Will you go along with me?" It's a challenge I find most pleasing, though I've not said a word to Mother or Father. Only with Eleanor have I confided my secret. She's most interested and I'm to teach her what I now know.

"If we're to be winter neighbors of these Savages...," she laughs, "... Indians, then we must be able to communicate."

We spend many hours together learning our simple words and phrases, whilst she suckles her babe. It pleases me immensely to be able to teach her. But while she appears satisfied to master a few words, I'm constantly craving to learn more. I don't understand why I'm so driven.

We're learning fast that this land is certainly not the paradise we'd dreamed of. An illness has struck our encampment, an ague of chills and fever that has most of us coughing and racked with pain. Thomas is confined to bed, as is George, young Ambrose, several of the women, even Father.

Strange that Eleanor and Margaret Harvye aren't afflicted. Mother thinks it's because they've kept mostly to themselves, busy nursing their babes and not mingling with the others. Mother looks tired and drawn, busy running from household to household to help with the sick ones. Finally, from his own bed, Father bids her stay at home and rest.

"We can't have you sick, Joyce," he coughs. "Besides, I've need of you myself."

He starts laughing and breaks then into a spasm of coughing. Mother fixes him a hot brew of honey and herbs, which seems to ease his torment. Later she makes both him and Thomas a chest plaster of mustard and turpentine spirits. The strong smell nearly drives me out of the house.

"If I'm to take care of Father and Thomas," she says, "then you must look after Eleanor and Margaret Harvye.

"Oh, I will," I promise and that becomes my job. I go back and forth between the two of them, helping with the babes, making them soups and teas, even bringing meals to Ananyas and Dyonis who are busy working. Then Roger Prat comes down with the sickness also and Dyonis begins coughing. Thomas is by now running a high fever and keeps Mother busy.

"I will send Towaye to... my people," Manteo tells Ananyas. "They will come with medicine for you."

What kind of medicine, I wonder. Surely they don't have physicians the way English folk do? Our own doctor is making his rounds, leeching those who haven't the good sense to tell him no. I'm so glad when Mother shakes her apron in his face for saying that Father and Thomas should be leeched. Oh, I've seen those black, slimy creatures he places on people's bodies; the big, purple abrasions they leave after he pulls them off. It makes no sense at all to leech a person of his blood when he needs every bit of it to fight off the sickness.

Strange, though it seems, I'm glad of Manteo's suggestion. When I go to see George and tell him that Towaye will be going, I find Manteo with him. They're talking in Indian dialect, though George keeps stopping to cough. I stand shyly in the doorway until Manteo turns and sees me. My heart is racing at his closeness.

"I am glad you are not sick," he says in his gutteral tongue.

"No," I find myself replying, "I'm too busy to get sick."

It's then that I realize he's spoken to me in the Croatoan language and I've answered him in the same manner. He looks at me with a long stare, but his eyes aren't cold. Then he steps to one side to let me pass.

"How are you, George?" I ask, laying my hand upon his hot brow.

"I'd be better without this affliction," he answers, coughing again. "*Connauwox*, I'm sick."

"When is Towaye leaving?" I turn to face Manteo.

"He has gone and should return at *oosottoo*, night."

Then quickly, the Indian walks by me and is gone.

"Oh, George, George," I cry excitedly, tugging on his

shirt. "Do you realize that Manteo spoke to me in Croatoan and I was able to answer him?"

But George is seized with a coughing fit which doesn't stop until I bring him hot tea with honey. He lies back on his bed exhausted, and doesn't wake until the late afternoon.

Chapter 28

A Very Sad Death

TOWAYE COMES BACK FROM CROATOAN Island with special herbs. He and Manteo make a strong potion for all our sick to drink. They boil it in a large black kettle pot for several hours.

It's an evil-smelling mixture, George tells me, bitter and pungent to the tongue, but it has eased his coughing fits and caused great sweats which have broken the fever. His clothing and sheets are soaked and Mother has changed the bedding many times. With ceremony, they smear a thick paste upon his chest also, made from the same herbs plus some others which are totally unknown of any of us. He's bringing up great phlegms which Mother says means his chest is clearing.

"Towaye is lighting stick fires all throughout the camp-site, Father, muttering incantations."

"What sort of incantations?"

"Strange chants which I don't understand. And he throws some sort of powder into the fires which makes orange and blue flames shoot out."

"Oh, Arnold, what do you suppose it means?"

"I don't know. Some tribal magic, perhaps...."

A thick pall of smoke lingers near the tree-tops but underneath, where we are, the air is strangely clear. Speaking in both Croatoan and English, Manteo tells me the smoke is to keep away the evil spirits of sickness which have afflicted us.

The two of them are wandering around the camp, making all who are ill drink their potion. Towaye continues to chant, sometimes calling for a pot of boiling water into which he plunges a piece of bone.

"This is the evil spirit which lodges in each sick body," Manteo says. "To put it in the water is to kill it forever."

The husbands have to smear the paste on their wives' chests; the wives in turn smear it upon their husbands'. Like George, all who've been coughing are now bringing up phlegms and their fevers have broken.

But sad news indeed. All this is too late for little Agnes. She was prone to spasms of the chest from her childhood and before Towaye even returned, she'd succumbed to the sickness. Oh, how Mistress Harvye laments, weeping and wailing. Her cries fill the heavens.

"Agnes, my Agnes," she screams out, beating her breast and trying to fling herself again and again on Agnes's still body. Mother and some of the others try to restrain her, but each time they lead her from where Agnes lies, she tears at them with her hands and breaks loose to run back inside. Poor Dyonis turns his face to the wall weeping in silent sorrow. How strange, how terribly sad to see a grown man cry so. He takes little Christopher and places him in Eleanor's arms.

"You feed him now for us," he says, his voice breaking.

"I'm still weak from the affliction and my wife's too distraught to care for him at this time."

Eleanor, her face drawn in sorrow and weariness, now suckles two babes, one at each breast. Mother says I must bring her lots of liquids to keep her milk flowing strong. Ananyas and some of the other men have dug a small grave near to where John Tydway lies. Mother and Mistress Steueens wash poor Agnes's body and dress her in a white dress that Mistress Harvye had among her possessions.

"That sweet child," Mother weeps. "She's dressed in white to enter the house of our Lord."

And I, how can I say how I feel? Agnes was like my little sister, both sweet and petulant as are all young children. She clung to my hand more than her mother's. It was I who insructed her in her letters, who sang to her at night when Mistress Harvye was tossing in a fretful sleep. On the hour that they bury her I don't go, finding myself instead at George's bedside, watching him sleep the peaceful sleep of recovery. His breathing is eased, his skin cool to the touch. I hear the lamenting in the distance but stay close to George, holding his hand and letting the tears run softly down my cheeks.

"You are not with the others?"

"No," I shake my head, not even turning but knowing it is Manteo standing in the doorway.

"Why?"

"I can't bear it."

"Little one," he says in his strange Croatoan tongue which fills my ears, my very being.

"Death comes to all. A bird falls but the Great Spirit knows."

Then he is gone and my heart is suddenly quiet and full

of peace.

Strange that I'm no longer *werricauna*, afraid of Manteo. Is it because I now can speak his language and understand when he speaks to me? My knowledge of Croatoan is limited, but my ear is keen for the new words and my memory excellent. All I need to do is hear a phrase once and *oonutsauka*, I remember it. Is it because I'm now a woman and have seen both birth and death? Mother watches me sometimes with a look in her eye I can't fathom. Is it pride as I pass from childhood? Is it because I've seen her at her most vulnerable and been able to comfort her, like friends do?

George has recovered, though he's not yet completely strong. Father coughs still and I'm worried, for he hasn't thrown off the ague which afflicted so many of us. He works too hard once more, yet has to pause in his labors to rest. Mother's concerned also. I can see it in her face. Once when I go to give the men some cool water to drink, I notice the streaks of grey in my father's beard. I've never noticed them before.

Roger Prat sends a company of men to the banks which buffer us from the outer sea. They're to report the passage of any Spanish ships.

"We must be ever careful to keep our guard up," cautions Master Prat and it's true. For when the men come back, they speak excitedly of seeing Spanish ships at great distance out to sea, plying the waters between Hataraske to our south and north to the Chesapeake. Father says the Spanish aren't giving up their claim to the Americas so easily. Though we knew when we'd left Portsmouth that King Philip was boldly gathering his Armada, we never dreamed he would actually challenge our beloved Queen and England. Ananyas and Dyonis both think we should anchor the pinnace left to us at the northern end of Roanoak Island, out of sight of any ship entering the sound through the southern inlet. Roger Prat agrees to the idea. Today, the pinnace sails to its hiding place and a meeting is called to discuss our future.

Chapter 29

Indian Medicine

FOUR DAYS AFTER THE MEN RETURN from the main-
land, a Spanish ship is sighted entering the inlet. Such panic
and consternation overcome us all. We quickly gather what
belongings we can, and Ananyas and some of the other
assistants lead us through deep woods to the northern end of
the island.

We leave behind most of our possessions. For three days
and nights we've hidden amidst the trees, the cold wind
cutting to our bones. We don't even dare to light a fire.

"I'm so afraid for the babes," cries Mother, making sure
that Eleanor has extra blankets to wrap around herself. But
Eleanor keeps them both warm, tucked close to her breast.
They sleep without much whimpering.

Fortunately for us, the Spanish ship doesn't sail deep
into the sound. It only weighs anchor near the inlet.

"They're probably taking on water and some provisions,"
says Father. "Or they could be making repairs from a storm

at sea."

To our great joy, they don't even sail forth to Roanoak but turn just inside the channel and head out once more. We rejoice that our pinnace is well-hidden.

"The good Lord has seen fit in His mercy to bless us," prays Roger Prat and we all sink to our knees in thankfulness. He sends scouts ahead to make sure it's all right to return and when they give the all-clear, we trace our way back to the encampment. But we wait another full day and night before it is deemed safe to light a fire. By then, we're all shivering and chill with the low temperatures of this untamed land. Father's cough worsens.

George says if the Spanish had found us, they'd have taken us prisoners and possibly killed the men. Who knows what would have happened to those of us remaining.

"You mustn't worry," says Father, trying not to cough, though I can see the worry furrowing his brow.

Roger Prat has said, "Love thy enemies," but that's something I can't do. We've heard such horrible tales of Spanish brutality, of rape and torture. I shudder not only from the cold but from my wildest thoughts. I give both Mother and Thomas special hugs. Even Thomas understands and hugs me back. Such is the uncertainty of our existence.

As Father's cough worsens, he holds his chest against the pain. Mother is terribly worried. She confers with Mistress Steueens and, in a moment of desperation, sends for the physician.

He comes the the next morning with his powders and instruments, probing my poor Father, thumping uselessly on his chest. He makes him cough into a cup, then examines the sputum.

"Hmmm," he keeps muttering, "hmmm...."

My poor father's eyes are sunken and his face gaunt. The cold days and nights in the deep woods have done him no good.

"This man will have to be leeched," the physician announces loudly, staring defiantly at my Mother to see, I suppose, if she will flap her apron at him once more. But she says nothing. I can't bear to watch as he takes the leeches and places them against my father's pale skin. I hear Mother gasp and put her hand to her mouth, closing her eyes so she can't watch. I squeeze her hand knowing that she, like myself, doesn't believe in such a procedure. But, in truth, she's desperate. The leeches stay on for an hour and when the doctor finally removes them, big purple and red sores cover each spot where they've been. My mother gives a small cry when she sees and sends the physician away. He mutters angrily all the way out the door.

"Oh, please, what can you do?" I beg Manteo and Towaye out of my own desperation. Manteo replies.

"There is a plant we have not tried before. Your father must be made to drink its juice. It is very potent and could cause him more harm. We must also build fires and cover him to sweat out the evil."

And so they set about finding the special plant while we light small fires all around where he lies. Towaye makes the potion which at first, Father vomits until he's able to keep some down. Then Towaye plays a strange sounding music on gourd-shell rattles and speaks many different incantations. We keep the fires burning through the night. Mother covers him with heavy blankets. She sends Thomas to stay with Mistress Steuuens and me to Eleanor and Ananyas. I weep the entire night, stuffing my fist in my mouth so as not to keep them awake.

For two whole days and nights, Mother has made Father sip the potent liquid. She washes him down and rubs a new foul-smelling paste Towaye has made upon his chest at three different times. Then she places hot cloths over the paste and wraps him again in heavy blankets. I make my way back and forth between our house and Eleanor's. Finally, I make Mother eat some venison stew that Eleanor has sent over. She sinks down gratefully on the chair and leans her head upon her hands.

"We may still lose him, Jess," she whispers, clutching my hand. "I can't go through another burial so soon. Not your father."

"No, Mother. I know he'll be well again. Listen, I can hear the sound of his breathing. It comes easier. And he hasn't coughed in quite a while."

It's true. Father's breathing has eased. We keep the fires going and pile the blankets high. At regular intervals, Mother forces the liquid into him. Each time, his tossing lessens and so does his spasms. On the third morning, he opens his eyes and asks for some food. Mother relaxes for the first time in many days.

"Tell your Indian friends that I'm grateful," she whispers with a thin, strained smile. I stare at her.

"I know you've been learning their tongue, Jess. At first I wasn't pleased. But it seems a good thing, after all."

"Oh, Mother," I cry, giving her such a hug that she can't breathe. "How I love you!"

Chapter 30

Towaye

FATHER'S RECOVERY IS SO SLOW and this annoys him terribly. He's forced to remain in the house now, for Roger Prat and the others won't let him do heavy work. It chafes him to watch the other men heave-to a large loblolly timber, or make fast our provisions for the winter.

"I can't stand this," I hear him muttering to himself. Even Mother's unable to give him comfort in this matter.

Our camp is still divided as to what to do. A great many men and some of the wives, too, want to take the pinnace and sail north to the Chesapeake. The rest are satisfied to stay here on Roanoak Island and wait out the winter. And of those, some wish to stay even when the winter is past and spring is upon us.

"I say we go to Chesapeake," says Father one evening, quite unexpectedly. My heart gives a jump and I think for certain, he'll notice.

"Maybe we should," Mother agrees. She turns to Dyonis,

sitting at our supper table with Margaret.

"What do you think, Dyonis?"

"I want to go," interrupts Margaret Harvye. "For, in truth, I've no love of this place."

Her eyes fill immediately with tears. Dyonis reaches over and puts his hand over hers.

"My heart bleeds for you," says my mother softly, and we sit in great distress for a few moments.

"Shall we, then?" Father turns to me.

"Oh, Father," I reply. "I... I'm not sure...."

"Give me my babe," whispers Margaret Harvye and only when tiny Christopher is placed in her arms, do her tears stop. She begins to sing a lullabye as she rocks him gently in her arms.

"I want to stay on Roanoak," responds Ananyas firmly to the very same question the next morning. "I plan to build my home here with Eleanor."

But she isn't yet committed to such a decision.

"Oh, Mother Joyce," she confides. "I worry so about my little Virginia and the harshness of this life. Surely we'd be better off in Chesapeake?"

"It may not be much better there," says Ananyas. "I hear the Savages at Skicoac under Powhatan are reported to be warlike. Here Manteo's tribe on Croatoan Island is friendly and amenable to us all. They've already brought us maize and other foods to help us through the winter."

"And Towaye's medicine cured Father," I add hastily.

But no decision is made that day, nor the next, and so we live, still uncertain of our future.

George, of course, wants to sail for Chesapeake immediately. He begs me to be of the same mind.

"I love you, Jess," he keeps repeating. "I can't think of

my life without you. You must persuade your father to make a definite decision. We must make haste before the snows set in."

Indeed, last night we saw snowflakes and today also, big white swirling specks whipped by the wind off the sound. It bodes a long, cold winter.

George continues to be most amorous and passionate, trying to get me alone to kiss and hold me. Though I'm aroused by his attentions, something deep inside me doesn't respond the way I think it should. I'm both in love and not in love with him. I find myself more and more not wanting to leave Roanoak for the Chesapeake Baye.

Towaye, I've discovered, is considered to be a medicine man, or shaman, by the Croatoans. He's a strange, silent man who shadows Manteo. But when it comes to healing, he knows exactly which plants to choose and how to prepare them. I want desperately to have him teach me, but I'm hesitant to ask. I don't know how women rank in their tribe. Perhaps my asking will make both him and Manteo angry. It's on the tip of my tongue to broach the subject each time I see them, but I don't.

A few days later, the weather turns surprisingly warm. The sun shines every day. Father is able to sit outside for long periods of time, soaking in the warmth and recovering his strength. One afternoon, Mother catches him chopping some wood for us. She pretends to be annoyed but I know she's secretly glad to see him up and about.

I finally get up the courage to ask Towaye about some of the healing plants. He's busy with his herbs and powders, for one of the younger boys has been taken with a coughing spell. I see him near the edge of the trees and, being bolder than my nature usually allows, dare to speak to him haltingly in his language.

"What are you doing with the plants?"

For a moment he doesn't respond, but keeps pounding the shiny leaves into a paste. I turn to go, feeling most uncomfortable.

"The young boy who coughs... it is for him."

"What will it do?"

"Ease his chest and release the evil spirits."

I kneel down beside him. He grunts and keeps pounding the leaves.

"Will... you teach me?"

Oh, such a bold and daring question. I tremble at my audacity, wondering how I have such courage. His closeness unnerves me and I'm ready to bolt. Many moments pass before he answers,

"You wish to learn...?"

"Whatever you can teach me of healing."

And so begins my tutelage. Towaye takes me from plant to plant, pointing out variances in color and texture, explaining as best he can what each one's purpose is.

"This," he grunts, "is yaupon. It is used to...to drink...." He pretends to hold a container and ripples his fingers to show steam.

"Like tea," I say, nodding my head.

But it's hard for me to understand fully, for my knowledge of their language is still limited to its infant stage and Towaye speaks no English. As with the yaupon, he pantomimes most explanations. During this time George sulks mightily and refuses to join us.

In these few short days, I try to learn as much as I can. It's a monumental task. Then I learn that Manteo has invited some of us to travel with him south to Croatoan Island and meet others of his tribe.

"Oh, Father, may I go, please may I go?"

I'm so excited, I can barely contain my joy. At first, Father shakes his head but then he tells me he'll think on it.

Chapter 31

A Visit South

I'M TORN IN TWO DIRECTIONS: weighted down by a deep depression that Father might wish to pack us up and set sail for Chesapeake, elated at the thought of visiting Croatoan Island and practicing my new skills in the Indian language. It's a time of strange feelings that need much sorting out.

Mother is very set against my journeying with Manteo and takes a firm stand.

"I'll not let her go," she states emphatically. "Mingling with a bunch of savages and she, of such tender age."

Father, still recovering, says neither "no" nor "yes." It's Ananyas who comes to my rescue. He hears my pleas and seeks out my parents.

"She'll be well-protected," he assures them. "I and ten others are also going. The change in scenery will do us all good. She's spent so much time with my Eleanor and our babe, it'll be a good thing for her. The Croatoans are friendly and freely offer their hospitality."

"And, Mother, dear Mother, I can bring Thomas with me."

Mother looks at Father. He nods his head.

"We'll be alone," he says solemnly, then gives a huge wink. "Not unlike the early days of our marriage."

He laughs, Mother blushes profusely and so, it's settled. Though I'm not thrilled about having Thomas tag along, it was a good suggestion for he, too, will benefit from such a trip. Mother lays her hand on Ananyas's arm.

"Watch out for her safety and well-being. She and Thomas are still young."

"Mother!" I frown. She glances quickly at me.

"They're still Savages," she cautions, "and you, my only daughter."

So preparation is made to set sail in two of the small Indian *ooshunnawa*, canoes. Manteo will accompany us and Towaye remain behind to offer protection against any unexpected hostiles approaching from the north. We're to be gone overnight. Thomas can't contain himself with joy and neither can I. George is coming also and even he's terribly excited.

Early the next morning, we push away from Roanoak and set a course due south. The men row steadfastly for several hours. Toward mid-afternoon, we see the shoreline of Croatoan Island, with its sandy beaches and stiff dune grasses. We pull the boats high upon the sandy, pebbled shore. I'm full of much expectation. Some of Manteo's people run down to greet us. Shy at first, they soon chat excitedly in their native tongue not knowing, of course, that George and I can understand part of what they're saying.

"Look at the one with hair of *heita*, sunlight," they call to each other. I blush and hang back at first, studying them as carefully as they study me.

122

Thomas runs all over, up and down, soon at ease with the younger Indian boys. They're sharing games within the hour. George and I follow behind Ananyas and the others, listening to Manteo greet each one and introduce us as his friends.

He leads us to his *oinouse*, or brush-roofed lodge and we spend the rest of the day in many sorts of celebrations. There's much dancing and singing, with words neither George nor I can understand. Manteo explains that it's the month of the "Traveling Moon," a time for gathering food for the long winter ahead. We sit on the ground, crossing our legs in front of us. Some women bring us wild game and fish they've caught and cooked, served on large shells obviously used as plates.

"Eat," he grunts in his native tongue, gesturing, then finally, dipping his fingers into the food. With great glee, Thomas follows suit, chomping most heartily. I see that Ananyas and the others are doing the same so I, too, dip my fingers and take a piece of fish. After a few minutes, eating from a shell becomes as natural as breathing.

Then Manteo brings forth from his house a woman much older than my mother's age. She has white hair, which amazes me because I've not thought of Indians as growing old like us. My heart leaps to think this is his mother.

"She is the leader of our tribe," he says. "She is called Shanewis."

Manteo explains that a warrior's name and property descends through the woman, not the man. She has no teeth in her mouth and when she smiles, it makes Thomas giggle. I frown at him but he pays me no heed. Shanewis doesn't understand why he's laughing, so she keeps smiling.

I pull Thomas close to my side, where he chafes and frets under my firm grip. Then two young Indian braves come out, for that's what the male children are called when they reach a certain age. One is younger than George and I, I'm certain of it, but the other appears a few years older. He must have been about twenty, though it's hard to tell. I only know he's Manteo's son and that Manteo speaks to him but I can't follow, the talk runs so fast between them. Then Manteo steps to one side and the young Indian smiles at me, flashing white teeth. Without thinking, I smile back then inwardly gasp, forgetting that I've received instructions from Mother to be modest. I can sense that George, standing next to me, is angry.

"Come," calls Ananyas, "we have many sights yet to see," and so we explore their camp and the surrounding area. George is fascinated by their arrows and hard, curved bows. He spends much time pulling back the drawstringed bow to feel its tautness. As for myself, I'm most intrigued by their communal lodges with the rounded bark and brush roofs and the drawings painted on the inside walls. As best he can, Manteo explains the meaning of each symbol. He sends his older son to continue when Ananyas and the others call him over. The son comes and suddenly, I'm alone with him by the lodge and I learn his name is Akaiyan.

Chapter 32

Sað Goodbyes

I'M OVERJOYED, FOR BACK ON ROANOAK once more, I discover that Father has suddenly changed his mind and now wishes to remain here. He tells us that he's still too weak for traveling to parts unknown. Eleanor also agrees then that Roanoak is the best place to raise her babe. She's very afraid of talk about the Powhatan tribes to the north. Though the Chesapeake Baye was John White's original destination, we're now so familiar with Roanoak. The island teems with small game and deer, and fishing is ours not only within the sound, but across to the far side of the land that stretches like the finger of God, protecting us from the wild outer ocean.

Our stories about the Croatoans are favorably received. They willingly offer us shares in their large stores of food and other assistance for the survival of our encampment. Their councillors, called *weroances*, have agreed to act as ambassadors on our behalf against the more formidable people of Secotan, Aquascogoc and Pomeioc. They've forgiven any previous frictions and offer only friendship. Ananyas reports to Roger Prat that the tribe of Manteo wishes us to remain here on Roanoak. They'll help in building a defensive palisade around our camp. Those colonists who want to take Manteo up on his offer are once again arguing with those who want to set sail for the Baye of Chesapeake. The camp is divided still.

George walks around in a foul mood these days. He's begged my father to go with Dyonis and the others who are preparing the pinnace for sailing north. My father keeps shaking his head no, holding his side even as he coughs. This illness has turned him into an old man, which distresses me terribly. Mother's now resigned to staying here and talks about the vegetable garden she'll plant next spring.

"You must come with me," George entreats every day.

"And leave my family?"

"But I love you, Jess. Surely you feel the same way?"

"I do love you, George," I speak firmly, trying to choose my words with care so as not to hurt him.

"But I'm too young for that kind of love. It's not strong enough to tear me away from my father and mother."

He scuffs the earth with the toe of his boot and I can hear the anger in his voice, which he doesn't even try to hide.

"You like the Indians too much, that's your trouble."

It's then that I turn from him, his kind gentle face, his sorrowing eyes. There's nothing I can say further to assuage him. For it is, indeed, a truth he's spoken and I've no words to tell him otherwise.

The pinnace sets sail for the Baye of Chesapeake. On board are fifty-four colonists who vow to see John White's dream of an English colony come true at its intended destination. Left behind are sixty of us, equally determined to make of this Roanoak colony a jewel for our beloved Queen's crown.

"Oh, I cannot bear to leave her," cries Margaret Harvye, flinging herself once more upon Agnes's grave in the clearing near the treeline.

"Come, come, my dearest," begs Dyonis, pulling her away. He hands her the babe Christopher, which she immediately smothers in kisses and holds close to her breast.

"Agnes, Agnes," she keeps calling, looking over her shoulder. Dyonis's face is wet with tears also. He leads her to Mother and Father. Mother draws her close.

"Think on your new babe," she whispers. "And on your brand new life in Chesapeake. It will be wonderful."

But even as she speaks, Mother's lip trembles and she squeezes my hand 'til I think, surely my bones will break. Mother then takes her favorite brooch and pins it upon Margaret's shawl.

"This will bring you luck," she says with a faint smile.

"Let me shake your hand, sir," Dyonis says then to my father, gripping him firmly. Somewhat embarrassed, Father and Dyonis exchange a fervent embrace.

"Keep our faith strong in Chesapeake," Ananyas calls, clasping Dyonis's shoulder and they, too, embrace. Eleanor kisses all the women and wives who are going, as does Mother. She even gives Elizabeth Glande an extra hug and her very own prayer book.

"Why, Mother," I whisper, "that was your special book of God's word."

"She has more need of it than I do," replies my wise mother. "Besides, you have yours and can lead us now."

For one last time, George takes my hand and leads me to our private place behind one of the houses. It's there that he kisses me long and hard, his eyes wet with tears.

"Stay with us, George," I say, crying also. "This will be a good place to live, you'll see."

"My heart's not here," he answers. "Though my heart is here with you, dearest Jess. I must go with Dyonis and the others. That's what my father wished for. The Cittie of Ralegh in Chesapeake was all he talked about."

"I'll tend his grave carefully and place fresh flowers there, just as I will for poor Agnes."

"I know you will. Oh, Jess, please change your mind and come with me. We can plan a future together. It's not too late to tell your parents...."

I shake my head. "My heart overflows with tears, but I can't. Though I love you, I can't go with you. You must fulfill your father's dream and your own, and I must fulfill mine."

He pulls away then, burdened with sorrow and the pain of leaving. I watch him go, my own tears mingling with the earth of this new land. Mother comes up and put her arms around me, drawing me close.

"My dearest Jess," she whispers. "It seems we're always saying goodbye to those we love."

I bury my face against her breast and weep inconsolably. Why can't I go with him? Why do I feel so compelled to stay here. I'm drawn to this place more than by my mother and father who remain, or by Thomas who grows toward manhood. I am... I am... but... I can't put into words what I don't yet understand.

Chapter 33

Akaiyan

"OH, WHAT AN EMPTINESS I FEEL," I say to Eleanor one afternoon while we're sewing. "I miss George and the others."

"We all feel it," she replies sadly. "I miss Margaret Harvye most sorely."

"Your babes were born only a few weeks apart. It's no wonder. You were much like sisters."

She gives me a quick smile.

"You're my sister, dear Jess, now more than ever."

This emptiness pervades our camp. Father walks slowly around, doing what few chores he feels strong enough to handle. Mother's face is drawn. She misses Mistress Harvye and her babe almost as much as Eleanor. Yet the three of us have talked and we understand how Margaret felt she couldn't stay here, for there was too much sadness associated with Roanoak for her.

Roger Prat is gone, having been asked to lead the Chesapeake group. Ananyas has been made our appointed leader in his place. Father says that Ananyas is a good man, both fair and just. Our colony will flourish under his steadfast guidance. It's my feeling Dyonis would have stayed also, if not for Mistress Margaret's longing to leave. There are several other good men who've elected to stay and make Roanoak their home. Roger Bayley stays and Christopher Cooper, and Thomas Steueens.

"I'm so pleased," smiles Mother, hugging Mistress Steueens. "I would surely have pined for our friendship."

"And your sweet honey tea," I add. We all laugh.

As for me, though filled with sadness at missing George, I'm still glad to remain. Eleanor and I, like sisters, share many joys together. Baby Virginia takes a great deal of our time and this helps in the loss of Agnes. She's now more than two months old and already, clutches her tiny fingers around mine and turns her head to watch me as I sing to her. I've spoken at length to Eleanor about my feelings for George and what his going has meant.

"Perhaps one day you'll meet George again," says Eleanor softly. "Life's given to strange twists and turns."

"Why do I feel sadness, yet sometimes I'm not sad at all?"

Eleanor laughs. "You're only fourteen," she says. "At fourteen, a young girl's fancy changes like the wind."

"I'll be fifteen soon. And I think that I loved George as much as anyone."

"George was your first love. There'll be many others."

"How many?" I ask incredulously, imagining a group of young men twittering like birds over a crust of bread.

"Perhaps there's one already," she hints, lowering her voice and looking mysterious. I stare at her, my face reddening.

"That wouldn't be fitting," I whisper, not looking her in the eye.

"Most true," she agrees. "You must keep such thoughts from entering your mind, Jess."

And she bends her head to her sewing, bidding me hold little Virginia and rock her to sleep.

I haven't told anyone of my thoughts of Akaiyan since meeting him on Croatoan Island that day. It doesn't seem proper to speak of the jolting of my heart when I first glanced his way and caught his eye, the churning in the pit of my stomach, the guilt I felt and still feel. I'd heard many wild stories back in England about natives seizing young English girls, mainly daughters of missionaries. It was always spoken of in hushed whispers, these terrible stories of lust and mayhem. But this hasn't been so. Akaiyan made no such advances while he explained the painted symbols, certainly none even akin to George's placing his hands upon my shoulders and leaning down to steal a kiss.

But like Manteo, Akaiyan's quiet manner has drawn me like a moth toward a burning flame. And like the moth, I can feel the heat and know it foretells possible misfortune, yet I flutter closer and closer.

That day at Croatoan, I felt strangely light-headed, very much aware of his lithe brown-skinned body near mine, his bared chest with its brightly colored shells of decoration, the soft buckskin he wore, his dark hair cropped close at the top, the rest pulled back with a single feather adorning. I heard his voice saying my name in his language, "Jessabel, Jessabel...," and it was soft as a bird's call. His dark eyes were depths I couldn't fathom, unlike George's in which was read all the passion of his heart. I wondered then and even now, what Manteo told Akaiyan of me during their swift conversation.

Perhaps George had been right, after all, when he said I liked the Indians too much. I'm at a loss to explain why I'm so attracted to these gentle people of nature. They're unlike any I've met before in my life. Their men move gracefully through the woodlands, blending into the natural world around them, hunting and killing only for food, never sport. Their women tend the hearths and raise the children, singing strange songs which catch my spirit and lift it heavenward. There are no boisterous ways to them; they know nothing of bawdiness and the lustful habits of mankind. Their rituals are simple, their laws uncomplicated. There's an innocence and beauty to them that draws me ever forward.

I'm a woman grown, yet a child when it comes to such experiences of life. I can't tell where the answers lie. I only know that I'm confused and unhappy, yet sure and happy, at the very same time. I'll be glad to leave this perplexing time behind, if and when that moment ever comes.

Chapter 34

Future Plans

IT SEEMS WE MOVE TOWARD OUR DESTINY, our lives becoming more and more intertwined with those of the Indians. Several of Manteo's tribe have crossed the shallow sound to bring us food for the winter months ahead. A thin blanket of snow covers the ground each morning, then melts quickly as the sun struggles through the thick November clouds. It's damp and chilly most of the days; the nights are even colder. Manteo's people wrap themselves in warm animal skins, a practice that seems most logical. Some of the women have taken the hides of the deer our men have killed and the Indian women have shown them how to scrape and cure them.

"A covering for little Virginia," says Mother one evening, displaying the deerskin blanket to us all, "and a pair of soft slippers for Thomas and you."

"Oh, your poor hands are bruised and scraped," I exclaim, taking the slippers and giving her a kiss. Indeed, her hands are calloused and have many scratches.

"No matter," she whispers. "I'm learning how to hold the tool more carefully." She glances at Father and there's a sadness in her face. "I am becoming quite adept, a true Indian wife.... Who would have thought...."

Several other bears have been tracked and brought back to camp. Their furry coats, *oochehara*, will make thick shoes for us to wear and warm coverings for our beds this winter.

Father hasn't recovered his full health. He still coughs and moves as if in pain. Mother keeps her worry to herself, busying her hands with cooking, sewing and curing the deer hides. Akaiyan has taken some of the boys, including Thomas, and is teaching them to string and draw a bow. At first Mother said no, but Father insisted it was all right. Manteo slips in and out of our camp like a shadow, sometimes here one moment, gone the next.

We're building a sturdy palisade around the outskirts of the settlement. It will provide protection should the hostiles from the north descend upon us. We keep a lookout always, in rotating shifts. Several more trees have been cleared to give us timber for the palisade and to enlarge our encampment. One of the women, Wenefrid Powell, is expecting a child next spring. Eleanor has confided in me that she and Ananyas plan to have another babe as soon as Virginia reaches a year old.

"I'm delighting in my child," she laughs out loud. "Ananyas and I want many more." She looks at me. "Does that please you, Jess?"

"Indeed it does," I answer. "Except when I have to change their dirty bottoms. I'll leave that task to you."

The absence of George has settled like a dull ache around the center of my heart. I feel he must be busy and happy at the Baye of Chesapeake doing there what we're doing here, rebuilding the fortifications, making of that place a new home.

Eleanor has begun a school for the few children who remain with their parents here. She's a good teacher, making them learn their sums and write their names and letters. Some of the children from Manteo's tribe have come from Croatoan Island to join her class. They sit on the dirt floor of her house while she teaches them how to write their names in the Queen's English. Mother sometimes comes and gives instruction from the Holy Bible, teaching them the glorious ways of our Lord. I am Eleanor's assistant during school, helping the little brown-skinned children hold the pen correctly and scratch their name on the slate.

I don't see a great deal of Akaiyan while school's in session. He hunts with the men and instructs our young boys and those of his tribe. We haven't spoken much. He knows little English other than the few words I've begun to teach him. I'm drawn to him by a strange yearning in me, as yet still undefined and vague of origin. Not yet love.... Perhaps I've lived before as an Indian in this strange, wild land in a lifetime other than this one. I share these thoughts with no one, not even Eleanor. As the days pass quickly by, I see the change in me from a silly thoughtless child into a woman of great mystery and longings.

Chapter 35

An Alarming Experience

YESTERDAY, A STRANGE INCIDENT OCCURRED which left me greatly unnerved. I've not as yet told Mother or Father. Perhaps I shall not, for they would sound alarm and have the men of the camp combing the woods from dawn to dusk. Still, I have taken my quill pen to paper to write down exactly what happened, so that I can sort things out in my mind.

I was alone by the stream which runs behind the outer ring of houses. It's a short walk down to those waters, a quiet place, full of solitude and good for meditation. I've gone there often whenever I'm full of turmoil, whether over George's entreatments or Father's illness. The sound of the water dashing over the stones is a comfort to me. The place is barren of flowers now, but I can imagine how it must look in spring-time, when nature's sweetness pushes through the warming earth to cover the ground with color. Sometimes I just sit upon the rocks which border the stream's path, listening to the water's music, hearing a solitary bird call out. Too often, I can't stay long, for Mother is always looking for me to help her with chores or to assist Eleanor with her babe.

It was early morn, one of my favorite times to go and reflect, for then the encampment is barely stirring, the children still sleeping close to their mothers. There will be wood to chop and meals to cook, but not yet, not yet. I was thinking deep thoughts of George and how he must be faring at Chesapeake, and of Akaiyan, who was more and more weaving through my mind. The air was chill and there was a slight breeze. I shivered and wrapped my cloak tighter about me, thinking it was time to go back for soon Mother would be looking for me. I was playing with a stick, drawing patterns through the leaves which had drifted down and carpeted the ground. I heard a sound and thought it might be a fish, but it was not so. I looked up to see, instead, an Indian hunter moving silently through the stark-limbed trees on the far side of the stream.

In horror, I stiffened and forced back a cry which rose in my throat. For it was not a Croatoan as I'd first thought, but a painted hostile with stripes of vivid color on his cheekbones and forehead. He was close enough for me to touch, it seemed, though in actuality he was far away, moving parallel to the stream and not looking my way. I sat frozen on the rock. If he'd approached, I doubt whether I could have forced my legs to move from under me, to run back toward the safety of our camp, to call out for aid.

I drew my body close down upon the rock, wondering if even that movement would attract his eye. But I kept watching him, for I couldn't take my gaze away. He moved like a deer moves through the woods whenever they suspect danger, slowly, cautiously, poising in his passage to search and test the wind. His bow was at the ready in his hand. My blood was

racing and I thought, surely, surely he'll hear the pounding of my heart. But he never looked my way and disappeared at long last beyond the strand of trees, ever deeper into the forest and further from our camp.

I waited for several minutes after he had left, hardly breathing. As soon as I thought it safe, I ran back toward our settlement, on feet which flew and barely touched the ground. I saw our houses, the thin smoke from our smoldering chimney fires, and dropped to the ground, giving silent thanks for my deliverance. Then I gathered myself and walked slowly to our house, to meet Mother at the door with a smile on her face.

"What a glorious morn," she said. "You're up early?"

"I couldn't sleep," I replied, amazed that I could even speak.

"Did Father's coughing keep you awake again?" she asked with a troubled look upon her face.

I wanted to tell her what I'd seen, to run and have her wrap her arms about me as she used to do. But I didn't. I will tell Akaiyan, I thought then as I went to help Eleanor with the babe. But I know I won't. The Indian brave never saw me, so engrossed was he in hunting. His build, his youth, indeed everything about him, reminded me of Akaiyan... were it not for the brilliant stripes of color upon his face. What if he'd looked my way? What if he'd come to sip water at the stream's edge? Might he have pulled a knife to do me harm, or spoken in words I couldn't understand? Would I have just sat there, or run like a deer or, perhaps... stretched out my hand? Oh, I'm dizzy with all these thoughts.... I should be afraid, but am only confused.

Chapter 36

For The Lyon of England

TO OUR GREAT CONCERN, Spanish ships have once again been sighted in the deep waters off those outer banks of land which protect us. They dip their prows and cut the seas in two, heading north, heading south toward unknown destinations. Ananyas has called a meeting of the men to decide what action we must take, should it become necessary.

"I say we strike the camp and head south now," calls Christopher Cooper and he's loudly cheered.

"We must not move in haste but if we do so, then we should head inland," responds Edmond English and he, too, is given rousing support.

"The war with our enemy, Spain, is surely becoming more pronounced. For what other reason do her ships traverse these waters with such arrogance? Vicente Gonzales, that rogue, sails with impudence and plunders all."

"It bodes ill for our beloved Queen. In truth, perhaps there's been evil done against her person and, even now,

Philip is standing at the gates of London."

The arguments rage back and forth: to stay or to leave, to sail south or to move deeper inland into the wilderness. The final decision is wrought not by the confrontation between Spain and England across the far sea, but because more painted savages, possibly Weapemeoc or Mangoak, are seen skulking through the northern woodlands. Like the one I'd glimpsed, their faces are striped with color, and they move with great stealth. Manteo says these hostiles seek out other tribes to plunder and kill. He seems ashamed to be of the same blood. I tell him that men of my world are also that way; some live in peace with each other and nature; others ravage and destroy. Perhaps it's the way of mankind. I've told no one of my earlier encounter, but with this incident coming close upon the sightings of the Spanish ships, Father is certain that Ananyas will call to strike the camp and move south to Croatoan Island, as is his intent.

Mother's very distressed and says we should have gone with the others to Chesapeake.

"We never should have allowed ourselves to be split in two factions," she laments. "There's strength in numbers."

"Our good people are having their own troubles, no doubt. The Spanish seek access to the Chesapeake, and Powhatan's tribes move constantly through the area. These are the dangers John White warned us about."

"Oh, Father, do you think George is safe?" I ask anxiously.

"Silly goose," he smiles, "as safe as any man could be. George is a Christian soldier in this new world. God will watch over him, over us all."

He coughs again and Mother's frown increases. Little lines of worry have begun to creep across her face, criss-crossing to make her appear much older than she really is. I run to her and give her a hug.

"Oh, am I still your own little girl?" I ask in a whispery childish voice.

She laughs. "My dearest Jess, of course, only you could make me smile so."

And so, the word comes the very next day from Ananyas. We're to pack our belongings, our precious treasures and mementoes, and row south to the island where Manteo and his people make their home. We'll all do so, even those who still wish to turn their heads away from the sea.

"A good move, for the time being," remarks Father, giving Mother a quick kiss. "'Tis done."

She clings to him for a long time, wiping tears from her eyes, then begins the arduous task of gathering our things. Under instructions from Ananyas, we're to take only those items most important to us.

We'll leave the bronze and iron guns, too heavy to move, and the chests which belonged to John White that he left in our good keeping. The men dig a deep trench in which to place his possessions, his armor, pictures, maps and instruments. After laying these things solemnly in the earth, we cover them carefully with canvas, place moss and branches, then rich soil on top.

"When he returns within the year," says Father, "we'll meet him with joy upon this fair island and reclaim it for England."

"For the Lyon of England," I whisper to no one in particular. "And for our beloved Queen."

Chapter 37

A Gift of Words

FATHER'S COUGH WORSENS AGAIN and Mother fears for his health. He's lost weight and now looks terribly aged. She moves around our house gathering and packing our belongings, sadness weighing heavy on her shoulders.

More and more, I'm assisting Eleanor with the babe. I rock and hum to little Virginia while Eleanor packs for both her and Ananyas.

She's told me that she plans to continue her school once we reach Croatoan Island. She's gathered all her books, the slates and marks.

"There'll be much to do," she says, making this statement of her intent. "There are many little children to instruct in our language and the ways of God. You'll be my assistant. Oh, how I wish I could take everything," she adds, trying to decide between household items.

"But you must pack all Virginia's little clothes. And the covering Mother made for her."

"Indeed," she smiles, "our babe has more things than either Ananyas or I."

"Mother has the same problem. There's so much to pack, she doesn't know where to begin."

"What about your writing papers?"

I clutch my journal to my breast. "I'll never leave any of these sheets behind," I avow quite firmly.

"And what's written on them?" Eleanor asks with a questioning look. "All the precious secrets of your heart?"

I blush.

"Ah," she smiles. "Then you must guard them most carefully and let no one read what's written there. You're lucky, Jess," she sighs, "to have the gift of words. It's a blessing from God. I envy you."

"You envy me? But you... you have everything... Ananyas, little Virginia...."

"I've watched you writing. Oh, if only I could put my innermost thoughts down on paper...."

The thought of anyone envying me is an overwhelming one. It gives me great pause for reflection as I go to fetch Thomas at Mother's bidding. As usual, he's with the Indians who are helping our men with the supplies. I almost laugh when I see him, for Thomas is so excited about the move south and has talked of nothing else but learning to hunt and fish like an Indian brave. Yesterday, he turned twelve but we had only a small celebration. In three weeks, I'll become fifteen. It'll mark the beginning of Christmastide.

I'm truly overjoyed at this move, though I dare not show this joy to Mother. She's so concerned about Father. I tell her that the Indians know of many other healing plants and cures. Surely Father will get better under their care. She frowns at me and shakes her head, then catches herself with a gasp, her hand flying up to her mouth.

Yesterday at twilight, I turned the corner behind our house while coming back from drawing water. Akaiyan was waiting there in the dusky eve. He reached for my hand and I gave it to him without a second thought. There was a vague memory of George but then it was gone. I stood trembling as he placed my fingers to his lips, his kiss warm against my skin.

"Little Bird," he said in his native tongue which I knew so well. "My father calls you Little Bird."

He turned abruptly and left, his footfalls so soft I couldn't hear him go. I stood in the darkening night and shivered against the cold, against the rhythm of my heart's quickening beat.

Chapter 38

The Promise

I GATHER MY SHEETS OF PAPER and store them carefully in the small chest I'm bringing, all my thoughts and feelings of these many weeks, going back to the time we first set sail. It seems so long ago, yet I know only a few short months have passed. I smooth the paper carefully, stroking each surface with my hand, re-reading each page. Oh, what a child I was when first we started, silly and impetuous, wanting my own way and no other.

Through all this time I've become a woman, known first love, then lost it only to discover another, sweeter kind. I've watched Eleanor labor and cry out in anguish to bring forth new life in this wild land. I've seen a man scream out his torment, then die. And a child, sweet Agnes, who now lies buried on the forest's edge, what of her? She'll never grow to womanhood, feel the surge of passionate first love, bring forth a child. I weep for her and for us all, who struggle to survive.

Father's still sick and I'm afraid he may die. Mother used

to comfort me about my fear of dying, but now she needs comforting herself. The thought of death fills me with horror and great anguish yet, in talking with Manteo and now, Akaiyan, I've learned that the Indians don't fear it as we do.

"There are two Spirits," Akaiyan has told me, "one is good and the other bad. The good one is the Maker of all things and does not punish any man, in this life or the next. But if a warrior be lazy, or a thief, or a bad hunter or any other manner of wickedness, he will enter the Country of Souls and face hunger, cold and troubles too numerous to mention."

It's certainly a simple philosophy and not unlike our own concept of Heaven and Hell. How I wish to believe as they do, that we're all a part of this beautiful land, this brilliant, vibrant wilderness! Surely when we die, our spirit will move to another life force. Thus, we'll live on in nature and be at peace with ourselves. There'll be no fear of dying, only a sense of wonder and fulfillment. I'm convinced that the "Great Spirit" of Manteo and Akaiyan is much like our own Lord and Saviour. We've a great deal to discuss and learn, each from the other.

Today we gather our belongings, our English possessions, and move into the small Indian crafts which will carry us to safety, severing our ties with that beloved land across the sea. Ananyas sets about leaving a sign for John White when he returns, so he'll know where we've gone. He's unsure how to tell him of those who moved to Chesapeake, so he's decided just to tell him we've sailed to Croatoan Island. The sign is a crude one, a mere carving upon the outer post mantel of our palisade with the word "Croatoan." To be sure it won't be missed, Ananyas also starts to carve the word upon the bark of a tall pine near the encampment, but is called away to assist some of the men. The first part of the word, "CRO,"

still oozes sap from the heart of the tree. He'll return later to finish it.

"John White will know to come and fetch us," says Ananyas and we're confident our captain will be back well within the year.

"He's a man of his word," confirms Thomas Steueens and we all agree. Surely our beloved Queen will speed his return voyage with our much-needed supplies.

Father's incessant coughing kept us up last night. Mother sat with him until she couldn't keep awake any longer. I found her early this morning sitting on the chair next to his bed, sound asleep. I made them both cups of steaming hot tea and then went to help Eleanor with her last minute packing.

"Do you think Father will die?" I venture to ask.

She looks at me long and hard, then places her hand upon mine.

"Your father won't die," she states firmly. "There are too many prayers wending their way heavenward for his speedy recovery. He just needs complete rest, for your mother says he's been trying to do too much regarding this move."

"I'll go then and say some more prayers," I get up to leave, "that is, if you've no further need of my help."

She gives me a hug and a kiss.

"What a good girl you are, Jess. And what a blessing to your parents. Go now and ask for God's intervention for your dear father and for our brave colonists in this new venture to the south."

I can hear her soft singing as I walk back to the stream just beyond our encampment. Strange that I'm not afraid to return to this place after sighting the hostile that early morn. Could it be that I sense God's presence all around? The sound of the water rushing and chattering over the stones is a comforting one. I kneel then, bowing my head and placing my hands together in silent supplication. The early morning sun shines through the bare tree branches.

Oh, Heavenly Father, I think, I come to ask your blessing upon my beloved father, and pray that You watch over us all...

...a soft sound makes me look up and there stands Akaiyan, a puzzled look upon his face.

"Why do you kneel and bow your head?" he asks. "Are you talking to your God?"

"Yes," I reply, so glad for his presence. "Isn't that what the Indians do?"

He flings his arms wide to the sky and lifts his face to the sun. The sunlight glints like diamonds on his warm brown skin.

"This is what we do," he says softly. "So the Great Spirit cannot fail to see or hear us."

I stand up, spread my arms wide like his and throw back my head to catch the pale sunlight. He sees that I've been crying.

"Oh, Little Bird," he whispers, gently touching my cheek with his fingers. "Do not cry... You will like living as the Indians do."

I take his outstretched hand and we stand there for a few moments, neither he nor I saying a word. I feel his strength flowing into me.

"I will take care of you," he says quietly. "This... I promise... For does not the Great Spirit love us both?"

It's then that I know I'll be safe... for surely I believe, in my heart of hearts, that what he has spoken is true.

Epilogue

CAPTAIN JOHN WHITE DIDN'T RETURN to Roanoke Island for three years. Queen Elizabeth I refused to allow any ships to sail for the New World while England was fighting King Philip of Spain and his Armada. Even after England won against Spain in August, 1588, no attempts were made to sail for Virginia until March, 1590.

John White was finally able to return as a passenger aboard the man-of-war *Hopewell*, accompanied by three other ships: *Little John*, *John Evangelist* and *Moonlight*, under the command of the same Edward Spicer. It's thought this venture was more concerned with privateering than in discovering what had happened to the colonists left behind. Actual arrival at Roanoke was delayed until August by their many skirmishes with Spanish ships.

Ill-fortune plagued their attempts to enter the inlet at Hatteras. A terrible storm came up and swamped a small boat containing Edward Spicer and his men from the *Moonlight*, who were searching for fresh water. Seven of them drowned, including Spicer.

Eventually landing at Roanoke Island fully three years

after he had left, White found no sign of the colonists, only an encampment overgrown with weeds, the rusting guns and his formerly-buried possessions strewn about and exposed to the elements. Upon the post mantel of the palisade he found the word *CROATOAN* and the three letters, *CRO*, carved upon the bark of a nearby tree. There was no distress cross.

John White and his men assumed the colonists had gone to Croatoan Island and set sail to find them. However, the weather was still unpredictable and the crew, under command of Abraham Cooke, could not be persuaded to continue on. Cooke thankfully steered clear of the treacherous shoals off the coastline and headed south for Trinidad, while the *Moonlight*, minus its captain, headed back to England. Of Simon Fernandes, no more was heard. He disappeared from the records, no doubt continuing his privateering against any and all ships.

Very little is known about the Lost Colony of Roanoke. It's thought that some may have joined tribes friendly to them, while others possibly headed inland toward what was later to be called *Georgia*. Further English settlements were established in the years following. Some Englishmen reported seeing Indian children with blond hair and grey eyes. The fate of the Lost Colony remains a mystery to this day.

**Follow Jess's adventures in the second book of
The Lyon Saga...**

The Lyon's Cub

Returning to Roanoke Island a year after leaving, the
colonists realize that Governor John White hasn't returned
with their supplies. What should they do now?
Can Jess and her family really make a life for themselves
among the Croatoan Indians, or should they try to reunite
with those who left for Chesapeake?

THE NAMES OF THE 1587 VIRGINIA COLONISTS

THE names of all the men, women and Children, which safely arrived in Virginia, and remained to inhabite there. 1587.

Anno Regni Reginae Elizabethae .29.

John White [Governor]
Roger Bailie [Assistant]
Ananias Dare [Assistant]
Christopher Cooper [Assistant]
Thomas Stevens [Assistant]
John Sampson [Assistant]
Dyonis Harvie [Assistant]
Roger Prat [Assistant]
George Howe [Assistant]
Simon Fernando [Assistant]
Nicholas Johnson
Thomas Warner
Anthony Cage
John Jones
John Tydway
Ambrose Viccars
Edmond English
Thomas Topan
Henry Berrye
Richard Berrye
John Spendlove
John Hemmington
Thomas Butler
Edward Powell
John Burden

James Hynde
William Willes
John Brooke
Cutbert White
John Bright

Clement Tayler
William Sole
John Cotsmur
Humfrey Newton
Thomas Colman
Thomas Gramme
Marke Bennet
John Gibbes
John Stilman
Robert Wilkinson
Peter Little
John Wyles
Brian Wyles
George Martyn
Hugh Patteson
Martyn Sutton
John Farre
John Bridger

The Names of the 1587 Virginia Colonists

Griffen Jones
Richard Shaberdge
Thomas Ellis
William Brown
Michael Myllet
Thomas Smith
Richard Kemme
Thomas Harris
Richard Taverner
John Earnest
Henry Johnson
John Starte
Richard Darige
William Lucas
Arnold Archard
John Wright
William Dutton
Morris Allen
William Waters
Richard Arthur
John Chapman
William Clement
Robert Little
Hugh Tayler
Richard Wildye
Lewes Wotton
Michael Bishop
Henry Browne
Henry Rufoote
Richard Tomkins
Henry Dorrell

Charles Florrie
Henry Mylton
Henry Payne
Thomas Harris
William Nicholes
Thomas Phevens
John Borden
Thomas Scot
James Lasie
John Cheven
Thomas Hewet
William Berde

Women

Elyoner Dare
Margery Harvie
Agnes Wood
Wenefrid Powell
Joyce Archard
Jane Jones
Elizabeth Glane
Jane Pierce
Audry Tappan
Alis Chapman
Emme Merrimoth
Colman
Margaret Lawrence
Joan Warren
Jane Mannering
Rose Payne
Elizabeth Viccars

The Names of the 1587 Virginia Colonists

Boyes and Children
John Sampson
Robert Ellis
Ambrose Viccars
Thomas Archard
Thomas Humfrey
Tomas Smart
George Howe
John Prat
William Wythers

Children born in Virginia
Virginia Dare
Harvye

Savages
Manteo } That were in Englande and returned home
Towaye } into Virginia with them.

FURTHER READING

Durant, David N. *Ralegh's Lost Colony: The Story of the First English Settlement in America.* New York: Atheneum, 1981.

Hoffman, Paul E. *Spain and the Roanoke Voyages.* Raleigh: North Carolina Dept. of Cultural Resources, Division of Archives and History, 1987.

Humber, John L. *Backgrounds and Preparations for the Roanoke Voyages, 1584-1590.* Raleigh: North Carolina Dept. of Cultural Resources, Division of Archives and History, 1986.

Kupperman, Karen Ordahl. *Roanoke, The Abandoned Colony.* Maryland: Rowman and Littlefield, 1984.

Lawson, John. *A New Voyage to Carolina.* Chapel Hill: University of North Carolina, 1967.

Miller, Helen Hill. *Passage to America: Ralegh's Colonists Take Ship for Roanoke.* Raleigh: North Carolina Dept. of Cultural Resources, Division of Archives and History, 1983.

Perdue, Theda. *Native Carolinians: The Indians of North Carolina.* Raleigh: North Carolina Dept. of Cultural Resources, Division of Archives and History, 1985.

Quinn, David Beers. *The Lost Colonists: Their Fortune and Probable Fate.* Raleigh: North Carolina Dept. of Cultural Resources, Division of Archives and History, 1984.

————. *Set Fair For Roanoke: Voyages and Colonies, 1584-1606.* Chapel Hill: University of North Carolina Press, 1985.

Quinn, David B. & Alison Quinn. *The First Colonists: Documents on the Planting of the First English Settlements In North America, 1584-1590.* Raleigh: North Carolina Dept. of Cultural Resources, Division of Archives and History, 1982.

Rights, Douglas L. *The American Indian in North Carolina.* Winston-Salem: John F. Blair, 1991.

Stick, David. *Roanoke Island: The Beginnings of English America.* Chapel Hill: University of North Carolina, 1983.

M.L. Stainer

On a visit to North Carolina's Outer Banks and Roanoke Island, the author became intrigued with the history of our earliest settlers, and the mysterious fate of the Lost Colonists of 1587. The idea for *The Lyon Saga* was born. What happened to those brave men, women and children? M.L. Stainer, an avid reader and prolific writer, happily researched the time period, interweaving fact and fiction into a fascinating novel. Educated in London and at Fordham University in New York City, the author holds advanced degrees, and lives in upstate New York with several dogs and cats.

James Melvin

James Melvin lives in Kill Devil Hills, North Carolina, where he operates Melvin's Studio and Gallery. He is well-known for his stunning portrayals of black culture and life. A versatile artist, he works in oils, acrylics and pastels, and has illustrated many children's books. He was commissioned by the North Carolina Department of Cultural Resources to paint *Raleigh's Venture*, a celebration of 400 years since the founding of the Roanoke Colony. Melvin's works are owned by collectors throughout the U.S. and abroad.

11751

EFIC   Stainer, M. L.
STA   The Lyon's roar

MAHS03955

DATE DUE	BORROWER'S NAME	ROOM NO.
	Bryan	
	Marlene Martin	
Oct 12	Brett	
	Tommy Lyon	5A

EFIC   Stainer, M. L.
F STA   The Lyon's roar
S

MAHS03955